stars
inside
her

stars
inside
her

lesbian
erotic
fantasy

edited by Cecilia Tan

CIRCLET PRESS, INC.
CAMBRIDGE, MA

Stars Inside Her
edited by Cecilia Tan

Copyright © 1999 by Circlet Press, Inc.
Cover art © 1999 by Linda Joyce Franks

Printed in Canada

First Edition November 1999

ISBN 1-885865-19-8

Circlet Press is distributed in the USA and Canada by the LPC Group.
Circlet Press is distributed in the UK and Europe by Turnaround Ltd.
Circlet Press is distributed in Australia by Bulldog Books.

For a catalog, information about our other imprints, review copies, and
other informtaion, please write to:

Circlet Press, Inc.
1770 Massachusetts Avenue, #278
Cambridge, MA 02140
circlet-info@circlet.com
http://www.circlet.com

CONTENTS

INTRODUCTION

The word "fantasy" has a double-meaning in our culture. There's the literary genre of "fantasy" where magic is to the story what the science is in science fiction, but then there's the colloquial use, where "fantasy" more often than not carries the connotation of 'sexual' fantasy, whether spoken aloud or not.

If you noticed the subtitle of the book, "lesbian erotic fantasy," you may have been wondering which of the two meanings of fantasy I intended. And I'm happy to say: both. I like my sex magical, my dreams sexual, my stories erotic and unbounded by mundane realities. Hopefully, you do, too. Because if you do, this book will be a treat.

Enjoy.

Cecilia Tan
Cambridge, MA

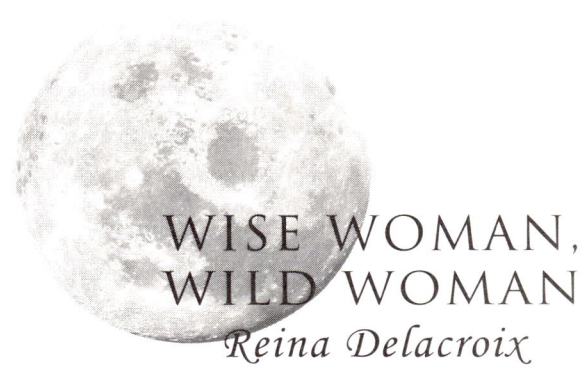

WISE WOMAN, WILD WOMAN
Reina Delacroix

The glade was girdled with golden trees, their brilliant leaves gaudy garments for the fall. Athena, goddess of civilization and cultivation, sighed with relief as she noticed a widening of the path at the top of the rise. The mountain forests were far too untamed for her taste, closing and pressing in on her as the sun set behind her. But a break in the overhanging boughs would make for an ideal campsite for the night.

She strode between two massive oaks that stood as sentinels to the dell, and halted, tilting her shield enough so that its device was invisible. As the keeper of the severed head of the green-eyed Medusa, she had to be careful lest it turn innocents to stone.

A woman already making camp in the clearing glanced up, frightened, her arms full of kindling weighted down with three thick logs. She was taller than

Athena, though nowhere near as muscular, clad in a white linen tunic cropped at mid-thigh and knee-high leather boots. Her midnight-black hair was pulled back out of her way in a knot at the base of her skull.

No, not frightened, amended Athena, just startled.

"Greetings, Artemis," she said in her kindest tone, to reassure the spooked wild woman.

Artemis's reply was hesitant but friendly. "Hello, half-sister." The wood-goddess stacked the logs with brisk efficiency inside the open flap of her large tent. There they would keep dry, even in the sudden thunderstorms that broke out on Mount Olympus when Zeus threw a temper tantrum. "What brings you here? You don't usually come this way."

Athena shrugged, the bronze breastplate of her armor throwing a few last gleams in the dying red sun. "Through your forest, you mean? I do, when it's the quickest route from Athens to Olympus. But don't worry, dear sister, I have no designs on your domain."

Artemis balled her fist and bit the knuckle. "I guess I'm not very tactful. But what I meant was, you've never liked the forest."

"The trees don't grow where I want them to."

"This is a forest, not an orchard," flared the goddess of the Deep Woods.

"Exactly," answered the level-headed goddess of Wisdom.

Their eyes fenced for a moment, Athena's grey and glitter-bright, Artemis's brown and deep-shadowed. Then Artemis laughed in her short, barking fashion.

"Exactly."

❧

Artemis showed Athena how to lay a cross-ditch fire by scratching a deep cross in the soft ground with a branch, so that air would sweep under the wood and provide a good draft. They pushed some of the first fallen leaves into the center of the indentation, then placed several layers of kindling, increasing in thickness, above the cross. Once the flames caught, logs could be added as desired at the top of the pile.

"Well done," praised Athena.

Artemis stammered, "I never thought I'd hear you say anything positive about my skill, half-sister."

"Why?"

The dark-eyed Huntress continued in her blunt way, "I thought you only admired the deeds of men."

Athena shook her head. "I admire a task well done, no matter the doer."

Artemis's moon-white skin blushed under praise. The blush deepened when Athena continued to be pleasant and thanked her for sharing both her campsite and her knowledge with someone who was, after all, an intruder.

"Not an intruder," protested Artemis. "Say rather a stranger... one I yet hope to call friend."

It was Athena's turn to blush, and to cover it she turned to remove her helmet, shaking her short, straight cap of wheat-colored hair free. The long sight of Artemis spied some coarser grey threads among the shimmering gold. "You have changed much, proud sister," she thought.

Athena set up the one-man tent she used when camping with the armies she assisted, while Artemis took her quiver and went hunting. She returned with a brace of brown rabbits to grill for dinner, and was skinning and disembowelling them expertly when Athena drove the last of her tent stakes.

Athena searched through her pack for herbs and an oilskin. "Here, sister," she instructed, "sprinkle the rabbit first with olive oil, then with these, to add to the flavor."

Artemis raised an eyebrow. "Don't you like the taste of rabbit?"

Though Athena would have preferred a leg of lamb, even a roast of beef, to the gamey taste of rabbit, she would not insult Artemis's generosity by saying so. "Spices should not mask the flavor of the meat, if properly used, but enhance it. A carefully added feather does not make the arrow stop flying, you know."

Although Artemis adored the richness of a well-roasted hare and was dubious that little bits of grass would make her love it even more, she was honored that Athena would gift her with knowledge. She knew Athena did not make that gift lightly.

"Thank you, half-sister," she said as she turned to light the fire with her stones of flint.

Juice ran down Artemis's chin as she bit into the seared rabbit.

"Hey, this is good!" she exclaimed as she chewed.

Athena hid her smile as Artemis devoured the rest of the meat with a fierce hunger, dropping the bones in a messy pile to her right. She herself ate neatly, clipping the flesh from the bones with regular bites. But when she started to crack the bone with her teeth to get at the marrow, Artemis cocked her head like a scolding bird. She said in a sharp tone, "Don't do that."

"Why not?"

Artemis cupped her hands around the pile of bones next to her and murmured a few soft words. Then, with a whistle, she scooped up the white jackstraws and threw them from her—

and a white hare twitched its pink nose as it sprinted away.

Athena grinned. "So that's how rabbits change their fur for winter! Man would explain it in terms of declining hours of sunlight triggering a replacement of the colored fur with white, so as to blend in with the snow." But she was careful to place the last of her rabbit to one side so that the goddess of Hunt and Hare could work her magic upon it.

"Man," growled Artemis, "does not know everything."

They sat in companionate silence for a while after dinner, as the fire burned low. Artemis asked once more, "So, what brings you to Mount Olympus these days, half-sister? We are very sleepy here, you know, more a hibernating den of bears than a bustling anthill like your beloved cities. Aren't you busy enough with Man?"

Athena had put aside her helmet and shield, turning the Medusa carefully against a tree, but her sword and armor she kept with her, eternally vigilant. She placed the point of the scabbard to the ground, rested her chin on the pommel to look into the fire, and sighed. The firelight turned her olive skin a flat brown.

"I am not close with Man, the way I once was. He discovers more and more every day, but he thinks of me less and less. Gone are the companions of my past: brave Perseus, swift Bellerophon, proud Achilles, wily Odysseus. There are no such heroes in the modern world."

Artemis nodded her dark-crowned head in agreement. "Man has forgotten my worship as well. Once in a great while a lonely woman will find me, at the uncharted verge of her barren world. Then do I gather her to myself, into the endless night. But for the most part I have learned to avoid Man. I have taken back my temples with creeper vines and crawling beetles. On earth, Man rapes and slaughters me. Here, at the foot of Olympus, I can remain inviolate."

"Has Man has forgotten all of us, then?" demanded Athena, her grey eyes flashing.

"I believe so. My twin Apollo sings no more songs in the sunlight; our uncle Poseidon slumbers in the depths of his beloved sea while Man spews his poisons above him. And the gates of Hades are barred and chained against the restless dead who have followed the One Father religions."

"And our father? Zeus? What of him?"

The wild goddess gave her a sloe-eyed look, like a wary doe, as she considered her reply. A staunch defender of their father, Athena had once turned the haughty weaver Arachne into a spider for mocking Zeus in a tapestry, and Artemis had no wish to anger her unduly. But it was her nature to speak the truth.

"Zeus rages at the ingratitude of the mortals, but his storms have little effect upon them. As they have ceased to fear him, he loses his power. He is still mighty, but..." She touched the tip of her index finger to her tongue a moment in thought, and finished, "The All-Father has grown old, half-sister."

"Has he?" said Athena half to herself, in a tone more of reflection than of resentment, and Artemis looked at her half-sister curiously as darkness fell without her speaking further.

Then Athena shook her helmet of dark golden hair several times, as if freeing herself from a net of dream, and excused herself to lie in her tent.

Artemis kicked over the fire with fresh dirt and stamped out the last embers with her booted feet. The moon, two days past full, had just risen over the horizon. She undressed to receive the blessing of its light, but their sympathetic bond was weakest while it hung like a bloated apricot at the tree line.

She had only regained a fraction of her power when dark clouds began to scud over the horizon to obscure it, presaging a storm. She gave up all hope of renewing herself fully that night. Even in the waning of his power, Zeus's angers were still a force to be reckoned with. Not wanting to draw his attention by drawing down the moon with the Dance, she gathered her clothes and went reluctantly into her tent.

The crash of thunder shocked Athena awake even as the lightning it accompanied struck an overhanging tree. The tree splintered down the center, through a heart soft with age. One half remained defiantly aloft, while the other half smacked full center onto her one-person tent and snapped both tent poles in half. No sooner was she fully awake than she was smothered by folds of sodden fabric.

She struggled free, shoving hundreds of pounds of dead wood and damp canvas away with her immortal strength, and emerged into the downpour.

Artemis's dark head popped out of her tent across the clearing. In the darkness she shone with the dim silver radiance of a crescent moon, her glow broken only by wisps of raven hair that had escaped from the pinned-up knot, so there was barely light enough for Athena to see by.

"Having trouble?" she yelled, and Athena could tell that she was trying to hold back whoops of laughter at the plight of a poor woodswoman who didn't know enough not to pitch her tent under a tree in a thunderstorm.

"No," snapped Athena, drenched instantly by sheets of cold water whipping in the wild wind. "I like being soaked. Any other foolish questions?"

The sharp-featured face of Artemis ducked again, repressed laughter tensing the muscles of her stomach until they ached. "Oh, well, I was going to offer the shelter of my tent, but if you like being soaked..."

Athena glared at her as she started forward, careful not to slip and add the word "mud" to her list of silent curses.

"Let me in, already," she shouted, and the flap pulled farther aside as the silver light receded.

Stars Inside Her ❧

The Huntress's tent had been constructed to sleep herself and three of the wood nymphs that were her usual companions in the forest, so there was plenty of room for Athena to lay her bronzeplate armor on the groundcloth at the low end of the tent. "Have you any mink oil?" she asked.

Always prepared, Artemis produced a small jar of oil she kept for boots and sandals. "Do you need my help, half-sister?"

Athena waved her away. "No, I always do this myself."

She stripped off her tunic and wrung it dry enough to methodically pat down the leather strips which joined the plates of hammered and polished bronze for supple movement. Then she poured some oil into one palm, rubbed it briskly on her hands, then worked it with her strong fingers into every inch of the damp hide strips to prevent overdrying.

So absorbed in her work became the craftswoman that she forgot her nakedness, and was unaware of Artemis's scrutiny of her body. Thousands of years of work, in the service of both peace and war, had thickened Athena's muscle on her already sturdy frame. Her neck was a straight column between her square jaw and her broad shoulders. Her left arm showed the massive overall development necessary to carry the heavy bronze shield which bore the snake-haired Medusa, while her lesser right arm (still stronger than any three humans') boasted much of its power in the wrist to wield her magic sword.

Muscle rippled over her shoulder blades as she pressed oil into every pore of the leather. Such was the development of her upper chest that her small breasts jumped in time rather than swung in rhythm with her arm movements. When she finished her task and knelt forward to place the last part of her armor on the ground with careful precision so that the oil did not smear onto the metal, the awkward position displayed legs that also bore heavy cords of muscle fiber but were less defined than her upper body.

Athena raised her eyes then, and Artemis waited for whatever comment she might make—about her study, or perhaps some mention of the moon goddess's own nakedness.

"Why do you always call me 'half-sister'?" asked the grey-eyed goddess.

Of all the things for her to say, Artemis had not expected that. "Why do you call me 'sister'?" she parried.

"Because we have the same father," replied Athena.

"But we have different mothers," argued Artemis.

There was no reply to that, save the steady thrumming of the rain. Across the deerhide blankets Athena remained silent and still, and Artemis realized her blunder. Where she was the first-born and much-beloved of her mother, Leto, the bright-eyed Athena was the most alone of the Olympians.

Zeus had swallowed Athena's mother, Metis, before she was born, and her preparations for her unborn child had given Zeus such a headache that he begged the smith Hephaestus to split open his skull. When he did so,

Athena had sprung forth, fully grown, clothed and gird-
ed for battle.

But Metis had not come forth with her daughter.
"I'm sorry, Athena, I—"

A flat short-nailed hand stayed her protest. "No apol-
ogy needed, Artemis. You asked before why I go to Mt.
Olympus. I go to ask Zeus to release my mother."

Athena had the bitter satisfaction of seeing Artemis's
jaw drop. "You have changed, indeed, to stand against
Zeus," she mused when she found her voice. "But you
shall not stand alone," the fierce Protector of Women
added. "I shall be at your side when you face the All-
Father."

"This is not your fight, Artemis...."

"Oh, but it is! If you seek to tweak Zeus's nose, I
must be there to help." Artemis's eyes gleamed with the
adolescent mischief she had never fully outgrown.

Athena's deep voice continued, stern as judgement.
"I honor my father no less than I always have. I do not do
this lightly."

"And I have always honored Zeus when what he
does is right. But it hurts me to see injustice done, even
by the mightiest of the gods. Yet you have always defend-
ed Zeus in the past."

Athena took a deep breath. "So I did. My father was
all in all to me. But I am tired, sister. The world I nurtured
has left me behind. Without worship and honor, I will
fade as you all have. If I must grow old—if I must die—
I would know Metis as well as Zeus. I shall bring her
forth, or die in the attempt. But I cannot ask for your
help."

"Athena, I once slew Niobe's six daughters to protect my mother's honor. I could do no less for yours...my sister." Artemis held out her hand in comradeship to the woman she had always considered a rival before, if not a declared enemy.

Athena reached out and grasped the slender porcelain-colored hand in her own, and leaned forward to kiss the pale moon-woman on the cheek, But Artemis shifted her body as well, and their lips met.

Smooth flesh that Athena had always expected to be marble-cool proved to be blood-warm. Compared to that, Athena's own mouth, flattened and dried by years of weather, was rough and leathery.

Yet Artemis did not seem to mind. She cradled Athena in her bony arms and stroked the short hair with a gentle hand well-trained in soothing women who strained in childbirth and wild animals panicked by death.

Athena found, to her surprise, that her eyes were brimming with tears. Ashamed of her weakness, so unseemly in a warrior goddess, she sought to bury her tear-streaked face in Artemis's thin shoulder. There was no pillow of flesh to rest on, not even the hard muscle that formed her own breast, but the unyielding strength of the Huntress was more of a comfort than a conventionally feminine body would have been.

"We have much in common, you and I," Artemis murmured as she pressed Athena's hand, smelling of leather and oil, to her mouth. "And yet our lives have been opposed. But you have only to ask for me to be with you."

She lifted Athena's face with one strong hand, long fingers grasping under the chin, and kissed her cheeks. "Let me worship and honor you."

Moonlight streamed from her; it played over Athena's curled body, beginning as a silver breeze that tingled and intensifying until the sheer force of the rays seared like cold fire.

Against the full face of the moon Athena's dusky skin seemed nearly black. Even the features of Artemis were sketchy lines on a background of blinding white. And still she continued to brighten, as her kisses followed the curve of Athena's neck, over the shoulder.

Wherever her lips had touched, Athena felt a tingle like honeybee stings, and she looked at her hand in wonder. A little of the glow of Artemis inflamed her own skin, a ghostly outline of her lips fading slowly as she watched it. A turn of her head gave a view of her shoulder dusted with sparkling silver, fading also.

And the parts of her body which were held in Artemis's grasp also tingled, only a little less, as if her skin had gone to sleep and now the nerves returned to life— to happiness, to joy, to the gift of being alive. The strength of the Huntress, hoarded in solitude, penetrated through her skin like pricks of a careless needle.

Had she declined so much? She had forgotten what it felt like, to be a goddess. She felt stronger than she had in ages, as if she could run even a race that would never end, as if she could lift the world with the shrug of a shoulder like Atlas. Her body swelled with the energy and vigor of athletic youth where swirls of silver caressed it.

Artemis was giving her a portion of her own divine essence. What could she possibly give Artemis that could equal this gift?

The cool breath of the Moon Goddess on her chest made her shiver. Even her nipples had come alive, hardening in response to the life that coursed through her, and Artemis kissed first one, then the other. Athena's emotions sprang forth with the same intensity of passion her mind had always displayed, and she made a last stab at regaining control of them. She grabbed Artemis's hair and yanked her head up.

Their eyes met: Athena's as hard as walls of stone, Artemis's as soft as valley mist. "Have I offended you then, my sister?" she said in a sad voice like the colorless moments before sunrise.

"When we were of equal strength, Artemis, we repelled each other like magnets touching at the same pole. It took my weakness to bring us close like this. Can there be no love between equals? Must one always be powerless?"

Even before she had finished, Artemis was shaking her head, the knot of hair loosening under Athena's fingers as she did so. Thick locks of raven-black hair tumbled down over her shoulders and down around her hips, dimming her radiance. "No, Athena. You are not powerless. You have only forgotten how to be powerful."

Athena blinked. Her eyes did not deceive her; there were streaks of shining silver hidden in the slender goddess's hair. Artemis was not immune to the ravages of time either! And yet she had given some of her divinity to a sister long estranged.

She tried to draw away from the other woman but Artemis would not let go. They wrestled, but even with what power she had gained from Artemis, Athena was no match for the fierce Huntress. She found herself pinned, with the cool hard body of Artemis stretched out on top of her, hands strengthened by years of archery pressing her upper arms down to deny her leverage.

With the increased contact, the power continued to pour into her, a sprinkle of moonlight rain increasing into a silver downpour. Her skin, parched, soaked it in until she felt as if she would burst. "Artemis, don't sacrifice yourself for me! I won't have it."

"It's not a sacrifice," said Artemis as she arched her back to reach Athena's left nipple with her tongue, giving her cold shivers. "I'm reminding you of what you are. Anyway, you can easily return the favor," she added as she shifted to lick the other breast.

"How?"

Artemis released her shoulders and rolled over onto the blankets, her body glowing as bright as a star fallen to earth.

"Worship me."

Athena smiled. "As you wish, goddess." She turned on her side and pushed herself up with her hands to look at Artemis.

In repose, her ectomorphic body looked to Athena like that of a boy at the verge of puberty, skin and frame stitched together with sinew. Her breasts were the kind of slight swelling boys have from the underlying muscular structure, her legs extraordinarily long in proportion to the rest of her body, as if the growth spurt had started up from her feet and not yet reached above the hips.

Athena closed her eyes for a moment, and concentrated on her own power. The gift of Wisdom, clear and bright like diamond that cuts through all other elements, coursed through channels long disused in her mind. She had forgotten so much—by trying to guide and teach Man, she had denied herself until she nearly ceased to exist. She had dimmed her own radiance so that it would not blind mortals. She had forgotten her true purpose, forgotten her divinity, forgotten herself. But she had not lost her gift. She shuffled forwards on her knees, carefully keeping her eyes closed and guiding herself by the intensity of Artemis's light that showed muffled and red through her eyelids. When her callused hand touched Artemis's leg, she moved more carefully and felt her way along the Moon Goddess until she could judge where her head lay by the position of her body and the depth of the radiance. She swung one leg over the prone woman, to straddle her hips while still kneeling, and leaned over to press her forehead to Artemis's. Wisdom flew from her brow, as spears thrown unerringly at a target, but she felt no diminishment by giving to the Moon Goddess, only the joy of her full powers returned and the worship of someone worthy. She opened her bright eyes to gaze into Artemis's dark ones, black and unreadable in her shining face. But the Huntress's smile was tender. "Blessed be," she whispered.

"Blessed be," replied Athena as she kissed Artemis full on the mouth.

Their tongues grappled, neither one winning or losing, but seeking within the other's mouth. Then Athena darted swift kisses along the neck and shoulders of her sister, marveling at the marble smoothness of her white skin under her lips. And wherever her lips touched, Artemis glowed with renewed strength.

Brushed thickly with moon dust, Athena's face tingled like she had been running into a cold wind. She nuzzled into Artemis's hair as she ran her tongue along the sharp collarbone, and her senses were enveloped by the dark animal warmth of the Huntress's raven tresses as she relaxed against her sister.

A thin hand slipped between her legs as Artemis received her weight, and only as her thighs were touched did Athena become aware that she was wet. Her body had always been numb to physical evidences of desire, and at first knowledge of her longings came solely through reaction to the pressure of Artemis's hand.

Then two lean fingers slid into her warm bay as the heel of her hand pushed up against Athena's mound, and started a rhythmic pumping that brought excitement rushing past the steely self-control of the grey-eyed goddess.

She followed Artemis's lead by placing her hand on the thatch of fur between the thinner woman's legs. The canal of the Huntress was damp and hot, and she moaned as Athena stroked her labia with nimble fingers.

As her hoarse cries deepened, her own fingers worked with double vigor, thrusting farther into Athena and building arousal throughout the dark-skinned goddess's thick body, until her muscles felt as warm and loose as after an athletic workout. Yet she strained upwards to push against Artemis's manipulation of her genitals—not to escape, but to increase the force rocking her pelvis.

Artemis pushed even harder against Athena's pubis, sliding a third finger in, then a fourth, and adopting a grinding rather than a thrusting motion. Athena's back arched, and she began to moan as well, her vision dimming as her consciousness drew away from the outer world and centered itself on the heat in her body. She cried out, "More, sister, more!"

She felt herself relax farther and farther into Artemis's hold, and as her hips loosened, thrust by thrust Artemis worked her thumb carefully in alongside her fingers. Athena lay on her back and spread her legs farther apart in response to the added width, and the Moon goddess shifted down along down the other goddess's body so that her hand could curl into a fist inside Athena.

Athena felt the blood pulsing in a vein that seemed to circle her vestibule, as the ball of Artemis's fingers locked inside of her and the slender wrist twisted slightly against her vaginal inner lips, rubbing them back against the swollen rise of the outer lips.

"Let yourself go," Artemis urged her.

All the energy that she had received from Artemis's kisses and caresses flooded her body in one vast explosion of light as she arched upward in the grip of orgasm. There was no stopping the contractions; though she tried to fix the moment by holding her body still, her muscles tightened and released in automatic sequence. Artemis lifted upwards with her imprisoned hand as well, and Athena half-longed, half-feared, to be torn open as her full weight balanced on the Huntress's strong wrist.

Once she had come and found herself intact, even strengthened by the pleasure she had just received, she reached upward for Artemis, eager to offer her the same pleasure. The shy Huntress, instinctively uncomfortable as an object of sudden pursuit, began to pull away from her, but Athena grasped Artemis's boyish hips, finding that she was now the more powerful of the two goddesses.

She kissed and licked Artemis's slit, the rich flow of sweet juice tangy and intoxicating, like a liquor of wild berries. As she sucked the flesh into her mouth, she felt the moonlight return to its mistress through contact with the hard nub she teased with her tongue.

Artemis floated several inches into the air and gave a cry of wild abandon as she came with a gush of bittersweet liquid that Athena drank avidly.

Before they drifted off to sleep, Athena asked, "Will you come to visit me in the cities, dear Artemis?"

She felt rather than saw Artemis flinch. "I cannot, sister. The world of Men is closed to me, lest I lose my powers. And I know that only your errand to Zeus would have brought you so far into the forest." Her chest heaved a deep sigh. "Once you free Metis, will we see each other again, Athena?"

The goddess of wisdom thought for a long moment, and then stated firmly, "We will, Artemis. We will."

In the first faint rays of dawn, Artemis' head shifted slightly on Athena's breast as they slept in peace.

Aphrodite smiled over them, then drew back to her the girdle of gold as she rose to depart on silent sandaled feet. She cinched it around her voluptuous body. When the lovers awoke, the bare limbs of the surrounding trees around them would tell them that, as always, Aphrodite had the last laugh.

As she passed the shambles of Athena's tent, she stopped, a glint of bright metal in the mud catching her eyes. Peering closer, she thought she saw an emerald in a fine setting.

As covetous of pretty baubles as a magpie, she knelt daintily on the canvas to draw it forth, surprised at how heavy the mud made it.

The Medusa smiled her serpent smile at the Goddess of Love.

CIRCLES
Stefanie Tatalias Phillips

"I s that all?" asked the convenience store clerk, eyeing the Cracker Jacks and Bazooka Bubble Gum. Or maybe she stared at my hands. Their nervous shaking began when the doctor entombed my heart, or more accurately my cervix, with the word Cancer.

"No. I'd also like a lottery ticket."

"Which kind?" She didn't disguise her boredom as a miniature TV screen absorbed her focus. I felt forgotten, unworthy of care, diseased. My frayed attention caved into Jerry Springer doing his best to incite violence between a woman, her husband, her paramour and his mistress. The audience alternately cheered and booed the sex quadrangle.

I wondered if I'd ever have a lover again. Who would want to get near my Cancerous vagina? Right now I would even take on the worst partner I ever coupled with. I'd allow Christopher to bend me over this counter

29

and force me to watch the porno channel while ramming me from behind. I'd let him talk crude to me and I'd relish it. Maybe that menacing long cock could kill the sick, traitorous cells. I'd permit Gwen to lay me on the dirty floor, put candy bars up me and lick me while I described the pictures in Playboy. Maybe she could suck this sickness away from me.

"Instant or Lotto?" The clerk asked.

"What?" I was a virgin lottery participant. The lingo was new, just like the doctor's medical terms. Malignant. Benign. Radiation. Chemotherapy. He pronounced them in a clipped clinical fashion, as if practicing doctoral elocution, as if the cleaner they sounded the more palatable they would become. This professional described cancer like a lottery, as he said, "Nobody expects to win it, nobody controls who gets it, but of course, people want to win the lottery." Was that medical humor? He didn't once touch me, let alone hug me.

"Instant or Lotto?" the cashier repeated and motioned towards a plastic case containing seven different gaudy tickets. She avoided my eyes.

I gazed with the dismay of a bushman teleported to the city. The selection disgusted me. I possessed no choice in the cancer department. I did not choose to legalize air pollution or artificial preservatives. Funny how the government does and then distracts us with bait, like seven different ways to throw away hard-earned money on chance.

What the hell. What did any of it matter now that the doctor convicted me of Cancer? I bought the shiniest instant ticket available and took my childish bounty to the car.

I drove aimlessly, with the windows down, in an attempt to blow away my pain. It didn't work. I began to feel like those filthy food bits left in the bottom of the sink after doing the dishes.

The hospital's sterile routine depleted my endurance. My morale felt famished and chilled. I required redirection.

I didn't think I knew where to go, but my internal guidance system took me towards my childhood stomping ground. Was it time to unearth my inner child? Was an emotional wound leaching toxins through my soul and into my body?

My auto pilot surprised me by bypassing the house I grew up in. Through the bug-splattered windshield I soon stared at a forest miraculously unscathed by development. Why was I here? Then my adult visor lifted. I used to play here!

Even though the fresh air made me cough, I dashed through the small meadow. My conscience stopped me at the tree's edge. Was I intruding? A huff of wind tickled the leaves; their laughter told me I was welcome.

Throughout adolescence this wooded overlock afforded a secret place for an awkward child to brood over her lot in life. The towering trees provided wisdom. The thick undergrowth's aroma infused comfort—and the security to teach myself to orgasm.

How many boys received my innocent spell from there? Back then I would focus one in my mind until I felt his hairless chest beside mine, his breath on my cheek. Our hands became one as I circled a spell around my clit and his heart. When I orgasmed, I delivered my apparition into his mind. The next day I would promptly receive an invitation to the school dance.

Senior year afforded new challenges. I discovered myself mesmerized with the fluid motions of girls on the dance floor. I sought the sympathy of the grove again. I consoled myself; if there was nothing wrong with me for these desires, then the Magic would work. Oh did it work! I fantasized that my friend rolled over to my side of the bed during a slumber party. Our hands reached for each others' intimate parts, while dreaming of our favorite pin-up. As we warmed to the physical touch, the veil of sleep fell away, thrilling us with the discovery of feminine flesh. All the while I fantasized, my fingers traveled in circles around my trained clitoris. The next weekend an innocent sleepover evolved into a series of intimate lessons.

The more sexual knowledge I acquired, the greater potency my spells contained. I knew my body then; I worshipped its reactions and its pleasures. What happened? I barely orgasmed anymore—with men, women or myself. When I left high school I put aside my mystical endeavors, my gender identity questions, and my promiscuity. I delved into a Mature Adult Life.

And now my owns cells, the building blocks of my physical self, were in revolt. If I acquiesced they would kill my spirit. I would die.

This Cancer was not just a physical emergency, it was a spiritual one.

I announced my return to the grove by singing and tossing handfuls of withered leaves into the air. My favorite tree stood erect, gracefully defying gravity and time. I kissed her puzzle piece bark and danced about. I tried to imitate her vibrancy, but my youth remained eclipsed. The decomposing leaves absorbed my tears like rainwater.

I resorted to prayer, supplicating myself to the trees' majestic power. I beseeched them to germinate some guidance within me. None came. Had I left the lookout too long? Had the trees forgotten my Magic scent? But trees are old souls whose lack of movement enhances their memory.

I crawled into the root base of my beloved oak, allowing the grandmotherly arms to cradle me. Unzipping my jeans evoked an embarrassed selfconsciousness. This girlish energy drew me back in time. I called upon the hours invested, the lost tears, the ecstasy. I gave my weight to the tree and let my mind climb away from the mundane. Who could I connect into this fantasy, who could fulfill my inconsolable need now?

Envisioning a God or Goddess seemed absurd, but I could conjure up a supple hand extending from the sky and touching me. It stroked my inner thighs, my buttocks, my hair, with a caress as delicate as wispy cirrus clouds. Upon fingering my labia the hair all over my body rose as if in a static electricity vacuum. My skin transferred its excitement to my blood, which felt pressurized like the air before a midsummer storm. The energy in my starving sexuality built like a thunder cloud. I relinquished direction of the fantasy. As fingertips began to bestow heavenly circles upon my hardening clit, another hand reached up from the earth and embedded my vagina with ethereal force.

Somewhere during the ensuing ecstasy the safety net of concrete reality became obsolete; my soul sprouted wings.

An orgasm sprang up my spine with adolescent vigor. It swept clean my despondency-disabled brain synapses and shot out the top of my head. The leaves of the mighty oaks clapped together, welcoming me back to the Circle. I knew then I was prepared for some real Magic.

When I opened my eyes the first thing I saw was my bag of comfort foods. OK Spirits, I told myself, I am ready for guidance, no matter how odd the delivery package.

The Cracker Jack's box bestowed upon me a blue, plastic airplane. I figured that one out; go some place. Of course I needed to go someplace. Somewhere, somebody would try to slash, burn and poison the unwanted growth on my cervix.

The Bazooka Bubble Gum comic confused me. There was Joe, safari hat covering half his crewcut, shovel in his hand, standing next to an Easter Island head. The caption read, "Hey this one's got tits."

I scratched off the silvery film on the lottery ticket. Five matching symbols shouted up at me, I stared blankly back. Over and over I flipped the card from the front to the back, confirming the imbecilic instructions. Magic was at work—or at play! I jumped up, hugged the tree, and danced with honest joy. Ten thousand dollars was a solid, thick, material cushion for my cancer crisis. The Circle was still my ally.

I reigned in elation to prevent fogging my vision. Application was crucial; the value of this gift was not to be frittered away upon premature joy.

I searched for a theme to the upcoming chapter of my life. I refused to be a lottery winner—or a cancer patient—who sank back into routine living. Airplane and money combined into a trip, that part was easy. Where and why? A vision unfolded when I accepted that crude language was not normally on Bazooka Joe's Bubble Gum comics. This one fell exclusively into my realm as clearly as the leaves from these majestic oaks fertilized the ground upon which they rooted. Those enormous, rough hewn, bald heads, left by mysterious ancient tribes on a lonely Pacific island, were not what they appeared to be. Or at least one particular sculpture wasn't like the others.

At the nearest travel agent I booked a ticket to Easter Island, Te Pito O Te Henua—the Navel of the World.

During the flight my resolve vacillated between inescapable confidence and perilous insecurity, like walking a tightrope right into the mouth of a dragon. Maybe that sounds drastic, but who was I to assume I knew how to cure myself, that I knew how to wield Magic, that I possessed insight into an arcane culture? I assured myself that setting the wheels of intent's vehicle in motion was the largest obstacle to any undertaking.

This first step was a big one; Easter Island lay two thousand miles into the Pacific Ocean from Santiago, Chile. Even from thirty thousand feet up the sea spread interminably in all directions. How endless it must have appeared to people in canoes. What motivated these ancient tribes to challenge this vastness, this vacuous saline beast? Scientists' dry pronouncement, overpopulation, bored my imagination. I sensed the story rooted closer to the eternal human quest—paradise. Be that peace, enlightenment, or eternal vitality. This last chimera lived in me now. I was a modern day pilgrim sailing the skies, searching for the fountain of youth on a denuded island.

🌿 Stars Inside Her

A heavily laden backpack rested in the cargo hold beneath me. Back home I had considered abandoning all my belongings for the freedom of travelling with only a fattened wallet, but that meant talking to people. I wanted to conserve my voice for dialogue with my soul. Besides needing solitude and silence, I hoped communing with nature would signal the Goddesses my sincerity.

The locals assailed me as I walked out of the airport. I shrugged off their solicitations and rented a jeep. Soon, I was alone with my mechanical steed, the barren landscape, and open dreams. I drove to what my guidebook claimed was a fairly untouristed camping area. The site appeared empty of people and full of possibilities. My newfound wealth couldn't have provided me a better haven than the spiritual shadow of the giant stone heads, the Moais.

My first night passed uneventfully. Exhausted emotions collapsed me into a twelve hour slumber. I spent the following day attempting spirituality. I began fasting. I meditated. I did yoga. Nothing happened. The clouds didn't write personal anti-cancer recipes. My body constitution felt no physical sensations of morphing into a healthier being. I wandered around the weathered heads, awaiting a clue. Nothing came. I actively searched the rongo rongo (hieroglyphic script) for an inscription, a signal, or even a token that I was meant to be there. I saw nothing. I prayed, contemplated and analyzed. Nothing.

The sun looked thirsty after its long day's work. As it dipped down towards the horizon for a drink, my emotional weariness compressed my heart. I felt lonely and scared. The cry of a sooty tern seemed to echo my longing. But she was a lucky bird; a mate joined her on the cliff. Their elaborate courting dance kindled an Idea.

I prepared camp for another masturbation session. As I rearranged the fire ring, an auspicious sensation that someone watched sent my hands trembling. I pretended to casually peer over my shoulder. I saw no one, only the lava-strewn landscape. The giant palms were long gone, eaten by the single-minded obsession to transport the Moais to the coast.

Emboldened motivations guided my hands. I wanted a proper Circle. I wasn't sure exactly what that was or why it seemed necessary. (The only conjuring tool I had dabbled with was my body.) For good luck I began clearing away bits of half-burnt camper debris, only to discover a round rock imbedded in the exact middle of the fire ring. I bent down to dislodge it. I thought a glimmer twinkled at me, but when I blew away the ash only a lump of dull volcanic rock sat there.

I tried to laugh at my desperation. What kind of miracle cure was I expecting?

Then I touched the rock. It radiated heat as if under the eye of a high noon sun.

My hands resumed their shaking as my eager fingers burrowed about the edges of this implausible treasure. The gift, the talisman, the panacea I sought! My arms quivered—no, my whole body quaked—no, the earth itself tremored as the rock heaved upwards and the earth cleaved open.

A giant stone head emerged. What God had I insulted with my imprudence? I closed my eyes and recanted my wish for help, but the sound of belching earth chunks continued.

When the earthquake stopped I opened my eyes to a monolithic body. That rock, innocuously sleeping in the fire ring's center, was actually the top of this hidden sculpture. The curving hips and full bosom alluded to something familiar, but angular shoulders and muscular thighs suggested a unique heritage. A women's clan on Te Pito O Te Henua must have created this enormous Make Make, their interpretation of the Fertility Goddess.

Terror and awe rendered my limbs immobile, but my stomach and heart competed for the most imaginative beat. Only my eyes dared crawl over this delusion.

My peripheral vision registered motion, bringing my mind into focus. I forced my head to turn to the right. A figure, bedecked with quills, wooden beads, and grass skirt stood just beyond the broken ground.

Were these two, sprite and colossus, apparitions of an infirm mind? Surely this unfathomable scene must be a lucid dream; the kind where you know you are dreaming but pain remains vivid. But I was awake and alert.

As I zoomed in on an oblong object in the human's hand, another kinswoman appeared bearing a shield. When the third one arrived with a drum, I prayed they were here to make music, not war. A couple dozen more materialized from all sides. What if my haste and presumption had offended this island's spirit keepers?

They held hands, linking the circle together around me. Their plumes and demeanor radiated the health of a flock of birds migrating in the spring.

Their narrow faces, angular noses and high foreheads mirrored the famed Easter Island heads—and the recently emerged Make Make. So this is what Bazooka Joe meant! The heads didn't belong to men!

They began to hum a sound as tender and delicate as the whir of a hummingbird's wings. Their warm aura evaporated my adrenaline. With their musical instruments and agile fingers they played a rhythm that was at once archaic and basic and infinitely detailed. Wherever they danced, the broken earth healed.

I did not know what to do or what to think or what was expected. I tried to root my being into the earth. That old saying thumped in my heart: be careful of what you wish for, you just may get it.

I fixated on my surroundings, allowing my bewildered mind to see a lush, tropical forest vibrating with life around us. A rising full moon accented the fronds of the giant palm trees. The arid terrain was gone. The time I came from was far in the future.

Two young women reached out, inviting me to dance. When we joined hands I felt a spasm arc up my arm, across my shoulder blades and down the other arm, as if we completed an electrical circuit. Inhibitions made my feet feel like tree stumps. The music, and my partners' lithe bodies, begged my embarrassment to depart. The rhythm inspired my feet and their hands guided my arms. Hope swayed my torso and hips.

Trapped body heat made my North American traveling ensemble feel like a Victorian corset. The clan's feathers and fronds swung freely across their butternut skin, easily revealing breasts, nipples, and buttocks. Sometimes a pair of dancers rubbed arms or legs or bodies together with the grace of love-entwined swans. Then they separated to twirl and dip and jump like fireflies at sunset.

Was I staring, or did the young woman read my mind? She lifted her necklace off her chest and offered it

39

to me. Another woman pantomimed that I should remove my shirt. She laughed at my hesitation and hopped to my side. Her fingertips swept across the sweat on my forehead, cheek, and chin. She made no hesitation there; her light touch continued down my neck and onto my breasts.

I didn't want to stop her, even though the provocation robbed me of the ability to breathe.

She shed me of my shirt. The other woman adorned my pink skin with the necklace. Her hands grasped my hips, as she stretched on tip-toe to kiss me. The narrow, prism-colored feathers tickled my nipples. I relished the mixed sensation of seeing her bare breasts and feeling my own.

Youthful intoxication—the joy of being innocent and naive and anxious and bold—drowned out lingering hesitation. I let my body loose. The music's pace erupted, as if synchronized to my spirit.

My hands encircled the necklace donator's neck. She felt like every woman I'd ever been with—I mean she felt so alive that I imagined she embodied the vital force of all the women in the world.

Her hard nipples found mine under the exotic quills. Our breasts orbited each other as our bodies gyrated in reverse unison. Electricity built between our chests as if we were generator magnets.

When she touched her belly against mine I desperately needed to rid myself of my shorts. Like a character in my masturbation fantasies, she automatically slid down to her knees while keeping her lips in constant contact with my skin. Her tongue flicked around my bellybutton. My buttock muscles twitched as if trying to shake off their confining clothes. I let go of her head; I was afraid of pulling her hair. I was not in complete control of my body.

I opened my eyes, not realizing I had closed them, to a fire built beneath the Goddess statue. The light played across her surface, enhancing her texture and deepening her ashen hue. The flames suffused her crotch with a garnet sparkle.

I looked down between my legs at the woman's bald head and beefy shoulders. She looked like a man, but probed the edges of my sexuality like a woman. Her hands slid to the small of my back and then angled downward, going underneath my waistband and curving upon my ample bottom. My elasticized, wrinkle free, khaki shorts fell to the ground.

I stretched my arms up to the sky, up to the Goddess. Her volcanic skin glimmered in the moonlight, could she also be wet with perspiration?

The gentle brush of feathers on my naked spine raised goose pimples, as if my skin wanted to expand itself and multiply the pleasure. I did not know who stood behind me. Hot breath on my neck teased my patience; my fantasies never played so long. I sensed hands caressing the energy field around my body. I felt safe and protected and ready to forget that anything evil ever happened in the world.

The love radiating from her hands turned inquisitive. I sensed her scanning my body and when she reached my abdomen she hesitated.

Her intuitive power hovered over my uterus. I hadn't felt the Cancer before, only various vague symptoms throughout my body signaling something was amiss.

Now, my cervix felt as if a foreign body was stuck to it, almost as if a toxic rubber dildo probed it.

The medicine woman made a satisfied sound and curled her wrinkled arms around my chest. Her hug could have lasted a lifetime, I felt so secure.

Then I looked up, I had to look up, as if someone controlled my eyes with puppeteer strings. The moonlight poured across the Moai's face, filling in the porous rock, enlivening her features. Her glowing eyes sought mine.

Urgent reflexes wanted to shield my half-naked body, but when I tried to lower my arms I found them immobile.

The dancing rhythm sprang into a frenzy.

The medicine woman had wrapped her arms underneath my armpits and then around the front of my shoulders. Her forearms bent backwards and her hands clasped behind my head. This hold incapacitated my arms. Before I could fight back with my legs, I felt my body falling as my mind tumbled into raw fear, stuttering a single word: cannibalism! Wasn't this aberration popular during the last days of this island's ancient society?

Insistent pressure directed me into the lap of a woman. Two woman took over restraining my wrists. Two others grabbed my feet, spreading my legs wide enough to incapacitated their muscles. The music was barely audible through my thumping pulse. The beauty who had been licking me returned to her kneeling position.

I wanted to scream, but she smiled at me in such a reassuring manner that I paused my terror.

A dancer stepped forward with something spinning atop a long pole. As she snapped the stick backwards, a giant coconut shell fell into the kneeling woman's palms. With reverence she placed the decorated bowl beneath me.

A familiar sensation swept through my heart's pounding.

The trapped memory of a one night stand, of rough play, and bondage careened into my mind's roadblock. It slammed into my subconscious safeguards and forced me to acknowledge that the adrenaline rush turned me on.

I prayed that the female between my legs was a friend. She read my mind or maybe our individual fantasies were magically linked in this nether world. Either way, she leaned forward and dipped her tongue into my bellybutton. A sharp warmth flooded into my clitoris. It spread into my lips and seeped into my groin. Like dripping honey, her heat sweetened my fear.

Still, my eyes were too afraid to unbolt, so I did not see the two woman appear on either side of me. Their hands slid across my midriff and came to rest upon my solar plexus. Their tongues flicked the feathers aside and latched onto my nipples. The heat between my hips hissed upward, towards their sucking mouths, like nuclear steam. My core melted, my resistance disarmed. My eyelids opened like emergency escape hatches. The dancing woman had reformed a circle around us and the Goddess figure. The light under the Moai's skin flowed ruddy as if with life's blood.

My "friend's" breasts were pressing into my groin and though I wiggled, my clitoris couldn't touch her skin. Her palms rubbed the underside of my thighs. Towards my buttocks she massaged, towards my knees she dragged her sharp fingernails for an agonizingly pleasing contrast.

I willed her to feel the wetness forming on my engorged sex. No response. I imagined her thumbs caressing the valleys adjacent to my mountainous clit. No feedback. If this was a fantasy, surely she would do as I wished.

Instead she kept titillating my bellybutton. As my attention spiraled inwards, I deduced the true meaning of "Navel of the World".

The bracing of my appendages turned from sour to sweet: fingers, cheeks and tongues immobilized my hands and feet with pleasure instead of force. The heat in my torso expanded exponentially. The desire in my vagina rushed into their hungry lips.

They did not consume me. They did not selfishly suck my pleasure away. They cooked it with ardor in their oven-like mouths and served it back to me spiced with their magic.

All this attention and yet no one stroked my hungry sex. I didn't need to fantasize a hand touching it, six woman adoring my physique provided enough mental stimulus. I needed physical stimulation. In desperation I flexed my pelvic floor. That heavenly figure eight muscle contracted. At first I closed both ends together, as if grasping at an imaginary face. Then I seesawed the sensation back and forth. My lips and vagina grasped at a phantasmal phallus. My anus pursed on a fictional tongue. Awkward alternation evolved into wavelike ripples. The swells of pleasure grew stronger and larger and, like a tsunami entering shallow water, a tidal wave threatened to crash out of me.

But the impending orgasm was not cool and fluid. It aggravated me like an unquenchable thirst as it burned against the frigid Cancer.

I stared at the Goddess. Her body looked like mine felt: pure molten lava, as if she filled from a deep fissure in the earth, as if a primordial volcano from the spiritual world erupted into her body. Coalescing red and black magma mesmerized my sensibility. Her vulva glistened fluorescent orange.

Everything in my mortal body felt inhumanly hot— except the icy Cancerous lump.

I suddenly felt an affinity with the Make Make. My need, my desire for help, awakened her from her earth tomb. Coming out of hibernation aroused her spirit's voracious appetite. I possessed something she needed. She craved to be touched, to consume human vitality. I could give her the crazed energy from my Cancer cells. Her fire could consume it; feeding her and neutralizing me.

The uncontrollable urge to expel the Cancer joined my cresting orgasm. My friend's fingertips curled around my lips and dipped into my vagina, holding open the ejection course for the Cancer. Seraphic lips enveloped my clitoris.

My fever ignited my uterus. My passion for life incinerated the Cancer's dominion. I orgasmed and the Cancer collapsed into the ceremonial bowl.

The shaman whisked it away, balanced it atop the pole and offered it up to the phosphorescent Moai. Her crimson, throbbing sex inhaled the sacrifice. The tumor's overactive life force fulfilled her lust. Her form cooled and solidified.

On shaky legs I joined the circle of women. We swayed and sang as the pacified Fertility Goddess sank into the earth.

My legs couldn't contain the weight of the experience. The woman let me sit down next to my fire ring. A few coals glowed in the center. My friend kissed me goodbye. As the clan slipped back into the jungle my vision wavered. The lush growth turned two dimensional, like heat rising from a desert, and then dissipated.

When I returned to the civilized world, a western doctor pronounced me inexplicably cured. I took a few more weeks off work in the name of recuperation and bought carving tools and a stone block. I needed someplace to hang the feather necklace.

SOARING WITH ELIANA
Teresa Noelle Roberts

liana had wings.

In some circles, it might have been a little over the top, but among the rather self-consciously trendy crowd we ran with, it was shocking only because she never mentioned it. If Michael could tell everyone about his Prince Albert (and believe me, he did tell everyone, in detail that started out as titillating and ended as dull), it was downright peculiar Eliana never mentioned the wings. The only reason anyone knew about them at all was that someone had gone swimming with her and seen them then, and she told someone who told someone who told the whole crowd.

With all the secrecy, you'd think Eliana thought she was the only person in Ithaca with a tattoo, which certainly wasn't the case. I myself had a red and gold Welsh dragon on my left hip bone (a tribute to my mother's side of the family that I'm sure my grandpa Owens would not have appreciated) and Celtic knotwork around my ankle (something to make the Irish part of my ancestry spin in their graves), and compared to a lot of our friends, I was mundane, only modestly decorated. Still, I showed them off whenever I could.

But Eliana hid her wings, wings that (according to the story that had by now achieved the status of urban legend) were true masterpieces of the tattooist's art, each feather so detailed you could imagine her taking flight.

And maybe she was wiser than we realized to keep them hidden, because those unseen—but imagined—wings drove people mad with curiosity, and then with desire.

All right, I'm cheating. I can't speak for other people, but I know the wings drove me mad. Even without those legendary mysteries, Eliana would have fascinated me, with her ethereal artwork that seemed like photographs from another world and her conversation that spiraled and dipped and dove like a hawk and always seemed to end up someplace interesting, with her long red hair and green eyes, her willowy body with both surprisingly strong, catlike muscles and surprisingly full breasts, her Burne-Jones beauty, her curious, archaic-looking clothes, and her past that seemed lost in legend even to those who knew her best. The unseen tattoo turned it from a crush to obsession, and, in the course of pursuing the obsession, to something that, if not quite love, at least involved real respect and friendship as well as raw lust.

The friendship was returned, but as far as I could tell, the raw lust wasn't. Eliana hugged me a lot, and kissed me on the cheeks and sometimes on the mouth, but she did the same with all her friends, female and male, the way some Europeans do. It didn't seem to mean anything romantic, and I'd never had any evidence that she was interested in other women.

Or, for that matter, in men. If she dated, if she'd ever been involved with anyone, male, female, or other, it was a deep secret. This wasn't so odd from Eliana. She never talked much about herself or her own past, so even I, who knew her as well as anyone in Ithaca, still saw her as a mystery. I went back and forth between imagining she had some tragic story in her past that made her shy of love, dreaming she had a terrible crush on me and was as nervous as I was about acting on it for fear of spoiling our friendship, and figuring that, due to some emotional or hormonal quirk, she wasn't especially interested in sex or romance.

It didn't matter. Eliana was my friend. I could talk with her, laugh with her, share music and dreams with her, massage her scalp and the back of her neck to get rid of her headaches. (Not to brag, but I'm an excellent masseuse; several of my friends call me when they get a headache instead of taking aspirin.) In my more rational moments, that was enough to make me happy.

It didn't always help at two in the morning.

Eliana lived in a cabin on a wooded hillside far from town. It looked like a place where elves should live. Dirt road, heavy forest (she claimed much of it was old growth, one of the few patches of near-virgin wood in the Finger Lakes), a pond perfect for swimming. The cabin had only had three rooms counting the tiny bathroom, but there were some great cross-country skiing trails in the woods out back, which ensured she got company even when winter made it fantastically inconvenient to get to her house.

It was mid-June, though, Midsummer Day, in fact, and it was unseasonably warm and sticky. Downtown Ithaca had been a steambath all day, so when Eliana suggested I come up and go swimming after work, I jumped at the chance. Besides, I mused as I raised a cloud of dust on the dirt road, it would finally give me a chance to see the famous tattoo. She wasn't likely to swim fully clothed.

Then again, she might. The clothes she preferred, long skirts and tightly laced vests over peasant blouses, or narrow, sweeping dresses that looked something from the early Gothic period, were dramatic and attention-getting, but exceptionally unrevealing. With my luck, she'd swim in a linen shift. I knew she owned such a thing; the times she'd slept at my house after parties, she'd worn it.

The heat, though, had forced her to make concessions. She was wearing a calf-length gauze skirt, one of her more mundane ones that she might actually have bought off the rack in an ordinary store, and a black cropped tank top I wouldn't have believed was hers if it hadn't been speckled with paint.

I had never before seen her wearing anything so, well, immodest sprang to mind. There wasn't anything remotely indecent about the outfit by anyone else's standards, but in all the time I'd known Eliana, I'd never seen so much of her uncovered. And there was something very bare about her bare skin. Even though she spent a lot of time outside, she never tanned or burned, and her skin was almost luminously pale even next to my Celtic-goth pallor. She looked like the heroine of a Victorian novel caught half-dressed, and that made her seem more naked than someone else would seem in the same outfit. I was trying not to stare, but I could see glimpses of the famous wings under the tank top. They were tropical-bird brilliant, stained-glass brilliant, and just as detailed as people said.

If I wasn't already obsessed with her, seeing her like that would have done it for me.

She hugged me hello and the feel of her skin burned into me. Even in the heat and humidity, she felt cool. More daring than usual, perhaps because of the tank top, I touched her a little longer, a little more caressingly. She made no move to stop me.

Emboldened, I began to knead the muscles of her shoulders—massage is such an innocent gesture, and such a good excuse to keep touching someone. She sighed and said, "Ooh, that feels good. I don't know what I did, but my back is killing me." She turned around, encouraging me to continue.

Eliana wasn't kidding. Her back was a mess. Every single muscle seemed to be in spasm. I could feel them twitching under my hands. The noises she was making were more pained than pleasured, but when I tried to stop, she said, "It's good. It's helping. In fact, I think I'll lie down and enlist you for some serious bodywork, if you don't mind."

Mind? I'd been wanting to work seriously on her body for months. This wasn't precisely what I'd had in mind, but it would be an excuse to touch Eliana and make her feel good. "Of course," I said, my mouth suddenly dry with anticipation.

She flopped down on the futon that was practically the only non-painting-related furniture in the cabin. Equally casually, she wriggled her shirt over her head and moved her long hair out of my way.

"They're beautiful," I gasped, looking at the elaborate wings revealed in all their glory. Not butterfly wings or angel wings or bird wings, but Eliana wings, distinctive and uniquely hers. The ends were hidden under her skirt; I guessed they continued their brilliant sweep down onto her buttocks.

I was afraid to touch her, I realized. All these months of anticipation, of fantasizing, were boiling under my skin, and I was afraid that she would feel my desire for her even through the most innocent massage. I wasn't normally inhibited about massage; I was normally the one trying to explain to shy acquaintances that really, I could work better on bare skin. But Eliana was different....

"Am I going to get a back rub," she asked mildly, face-down on a batik pillow, "or did you melt in the heat?"

Taking a deep breath, I straddled her hips (trying not to think of how often I'd contemplated doing so in another context, with Eliana lying on her back rather than her stomach) and started to work on her knotted muscles.

I repeated to myself *cool, friendly, affectionate but not sexual*, but as my hands moved over her smooth, decorated skin, I kept having to adjust my weight so she wouldn't feel the moisture soaking through my shorts. She smelled of spice and roses. I did my best to ignore it.

I resolutely kneaded and pummeled and stroked the spasming, colorful back. I resolutely did not let my hands stray below her waist or around toward the curve of her breasts, although I would have on someone less dangerously attractive. But I indulged myself this much: with my fingers I traced the outlines of the feathers, the lines where colors met and blurred from shade to shade.

At first, Eliana sighed and made contented noises, every once in a while grunting when I released an especially vile knot. After twenty minutes or so (I was dripping sweat, but wasn't about to stop until ordered) her breathing changed, and I realized she was either asleep or in that happily altered state of consciousness where a good massage can send you. Curiously, her muscles seemed just as tense as ever, despite my good work. In a couple of places, I could actually see the knots under her skin, accentuated by the colors of the tattoo. Eliana, however, seemed completely relaxed, oblivious to everything.

What I did then was, strictly speaking, rude. It was nothing drastic, but it wasn't fair to invade her drowsy privacy. But she looked so beautiful lying there, and it wasn't as if she were comatose and helpless. At any second, she could wake up and, if so inclined, slap me silly. And there is only so much frustration the human libido can take.

I wet two fingers in my mouth and traced the outline of the tattooed wings, still staying above the waistband of her skirt. When the moist touch didn't seem to disturb her, I let my tongue follow the path my fingers had marked. She sighed, but did not protest, or even wake up. She tasted like sun and spiderwebs jeweled with dew, like good burgundy, like the most beautiful, desirable person I'd ever met. Emboldened and apparently hallucinating from heat and lust, for I swore I saw a pulsing blue light where my tongue had passed, I embarked upon the notable project of kissing each and every feather of her tattoo.

Her skin was twitching, all but leaping under my lips.

Just my overheated imagination, surely.

Then a feather tickled my nose.

I jumped and took a good look.

The tattoo wings were sprouting in soft, feathery waves from Eliana's back.

If I'd ever done acid, I would have figured I was having a flashback, but I never had. Gingerly, I let one fingertip stroke a feather. It was tickly, slightly warm, decidedly real. I shrieked and threw myself off Eliana.

Eliana rolled over, sat up, and smiled at me. Her eyes were more green than ever, more green than eyes have a right to be, and huge wings of teal and purple and gold spread out behind her. "It took you long enough, Mari. I've wanted you for months and months," she said calmly, as if that were what mattered, that and not the wings or the unearthly light of her eyes.

And she reached out her small, elegant white hands and suddenly that was what mattered. She pulled me onto her lap with surprisingly little effort (mind you, I wasn't fighting), and her arms folded around me.

We kissed, really kissed, for the first time. Her skin was cool, but her mouth was hot against mine and her little hands had already slipped under my shirt. After months of seeming shyness, she was bolder than I, slipping her tongue into my mouth before I dared, caressing my breasts while I was still dealing with the safe, public territory of back, and arms, and throat. Once in a while I would brush her wings and shiver a little, but it wasn't from fear, just from one more sensation toying with my overextended senses. And when I bent down and took one of her large, rosy nipples in my mouth at last, her wings folded around me, feathers upon feathers caressing my overstimulated skin. I thought an angel was carrying me to heaven by the express train.

In retrospect, I suppose I should have been scared witless, and maybe I was under the dangerous surges of desire. But all I knew was that I was making love at last to the beautiful, brilliant woman I'd desired for over a year and the gently nipping teeth at my throat and the hands sliding from my breasts to my thighs and back again suggested she was at least as in lust as I was. The whole thing had such a miraculous aspect to it that Eliana's wings didn't seem that odd, at least to my hormone-fogged brain.

First one nipple, then the other. Her breasts were ridiculous, delicious, as phantasmal and unlikely as her wings, an extravagance of flesh on her slender body. I suckled at them until she squirmed and begged for more.

This sounded like a fine idea. I would have been doing the same if my mouth hadn't been otherwise occupied, and if I hadn't been too enthralled to rush the proceedings. I relieved her of her rumpled skirt and her underpants (plain white cotton hipsters, and I suspect I'll always have a soft and decidedly moist spot for such unassuming panties). She relieved me of my thoroughly damp shorts and equally damp panties (also cotton hip-sters, but leopard-spotted). She paused to admire and nibble on my dragon. To my relief, it did not burst out of my hipbone, but inside me, I felt it spread its wings and roar delicious fire.

All this newly-bared skin meant we had more exploring to do. I kissed the backs of her knees and drew Celtic spirals with my tongue on her smooth ass, her wings tickling the back of my neck all the while, and discovered with some disappointment that she was too tick-lish to enjoy having her toes sucked. She teased the drag-on, kissed down my thighs and back up them again, teased the dragon some more, outlined the knotwork on my ankle and matched it on the other side. Her wings were wonderfully articulated, agile. They moved over my flesh as gracefully as her hands did, with a more delicate but equally devastating effect, dipping down my belly, just brushing between my legs. She licked the moisture off my thighs, but didn't follow it back to its source. I squirmed and begged and tried to encourage her in the right direction, but she smiled evilly and continued to tease.

Somehow when I'd fantasized about Eliana, I'd always seen myself as the aggressor, making love to her, tasting her fire-haired pussy, opening her gently with my fingers, or not so gently if she wanted it that way. She seemed so innocent, so ethereal, that I hadn't been able to imagine her reciprocating, and in my fantasies, at least, it hadn't mattered. Even in my fantasies, I'm not what you'd call butch by any stretch of the imagination, but Eliana's seeming fragility brought out that streak in me.

Which was why I was a little surprised to find myself literally forced back onto the futon with my wrists pinned down with a strength that surprised and aroused me, Eliana's glossy red head between my legs and a pointy, not-exactly-human tongue playing music on my clit. I did what any self-respecting bisexual female would do under the circumstances. I said something truly articulate like, "Oh, yes!" and let her tongue work its magic. She let go of my wrists after a little while, and I twisted my hands in the sheets to keep from clawing her delicate skin. Her wings caressed my breasts, stroked down my belly, tickled my thighs.

I was bucking and moaning incoherently and probably would have been alarming the neighbors if Eliana had any. I came almost immediately, but Eliana didn't stop.

A feathery touch stroked my labia, teased backwards, then forwards again. Repeated, this time with a little pressure behind it... and again... again... and all the while her mouth worked on me.

Then the wing tip entered me.

I became a human hurricane, tornado, force of nature, as she brought me to a place somewhere beyond great sex and close to spiritual truth that no one's tongue or fingers or penis had helped me reach before. I've always believed that sex could be, should be, a sacred mystery. This time, it was.

Finally, she let me come back to myself. I lay stunned for a while, panting, hardly aware of myself, but very aware of Eliana curled up with her head on my hip. All I could do for a long time was stroke her hair and make little happy-animal noises. But once I caught my breath and found a few still-functional brain cells, I wanted, no, needed, to return the pleasure she had given me.

I scooted down a little and she scooted up a little and with a little bit of giggled direction, she ended up kneeling over my mouth. Perfect—I love being beneath someone that way, having her move against my face easily as I make love to her. She hesitated for a second, so I put my hands on her hips and guided her down to me.

She tasted like no woman I'd ever been with, and certainly like no man. Something wild and ancient of the woodland and sky and bright dreaming, something like the primal root of all sex, something with spice and roses. Her cries were silvery, birdlike, but she felt more like a baby seal playing in deliciously flavored olive oil. I licked gently at first, delicately, until she ground herself against me and delicacy wasn't an option anymore. I pressed two fingers into her and she clenched around them, sucking her breath in between her teeth. I wanted to crawl inside her and stay forever, and she was trying to pull me in so I could. Her wings beat upon me as she came and came.

Then, because one of the delightful things about being with another woman is that it's possible to "repeat until completely exhausted," we did. Eliana lying on top of me, we kissed to utter delirium and rubbed our slippery bodies together until our mouths captured the other's cries. We moved side by side, head to groin, tasted each other again. We spent what seemed like hours just stroking each other and talking about nothing in particular, then fell on each other again.

Finally, I lay surrounded by Eliana's bright wings as we huddled on the driest bit of futon we could find. I almost drifted off to sleep before I thought to ask, "I don't mean to be nosy, but ..."

She laughed like silver bells and answered the question before I could finish it. "I am of the Tuatha de Danaan." I nodded. "I thought you would know the old name, Mari my heart. I am not one of the great ones of the High Court, the ones in the fantasy novels you like to read. My kind do not have their strength of magic, or their near-immortality, or their coldness. We are closer to your kind—we can be as passionate and woolly-headed and emotional as any human, and like you, we can make art. That was always our role under the Hills. That and showing off a bit, because grand and powerful as the High Court are, they don't have these." She shook her wings lightly.

"Why didn't I see the wings before?"

She kissed me before she answered. "Because they were hidden, my heart. I am very young for one of my people, and among my people, the blossoming of the wings is the last sign of adulthood, of sexual maturity. And before you ask—" she tweaked my nose gently, affectionately "—I was a late bloomer. Still, it isn't uncommon for someone to be fully adult in other ways and still somewhat asexual. We need the spark, the desire of another of the Fair Folk whom we in turn desire, and there are so few of us in America.... I'd been feeling my wings throbbing under my skin forever, every time you were near me, but you didn't seem interested. You touched me less than you did casual acquaintances."

"I was afraid of scaring you away!" I laughed. Then something she said struck me. "But you said you needed one of your people. I'm just an ordinary human."

"Hardly ordinary." Her smile could only be described as a satisfied smirk. I liked to see it. "And I hate to break it to you, no more than part human. Your family is Welsh, isn't it?" She stroked the dragon tattoo on my hip.

"And Irish and French."

"Breton, I would imagine."

I nodded. I'd never told her or anyone in our crowd that one of my great-grandmothers was born practically in the shadow of a circle of standing stones in Brittany, but it didn't surprise me that she knew.

"People from all those places have traces of our blood. In some, it shows up more strongly than in others. I guess it was enough." She gave another of her silvery laughs. "It must have been. I'm here. You're here. They're here." She flicked one wing indolently.

"And they're lovely." I demonstrated for a moment just how lovely I found them, and her. "But how are you going to explain this to everyone else?"

"I'm not. Wings are a little much even for liberal Ithaca, but now that I've come into my full powers, I can just do this." She closed her eyes and screwed up her face with concentration.

The wings folded back into the complicated tattoo they had appeared to be. I couldn't even feel them anymore. Without them, I felt lonely and somehow, despite the heat, cold. As if she read my mind—and being what she was, she probably did—she blinked twice. The wings remained invisible, but I could feel them again, holding me close and safe. "You're the only one who will know, Mari. Only you."

"I'll keep your secret," I said, and not because I feared her powers (although coming from a family of wild-eyed Celts, I knew about the powers of the Tuatha de Danaan, and how serious they were about keeping secrets), but because I loved her. Before I could finish the sentence, she covered my mouth with hers.

Eventually, we fell asleep, or I did at least. When I woke again, moonlight was pouring through the picture window. Eliana was naked and shimmering in the silvery light. I walked up to her. She stepped behind me, embraced me with both arms and wings from behind and rested her head on my shoulder. We settled back to watch the full moon together.

Hyperaware of her, I could feel her body had subtly changed. I'd always realized she was strong for someone so slender and seemingly delicate, but now I could feel velvet-clothed iron in her. At the same time, she seemed both more otherworldly and more sensual, more pre-Raphaelite than ever. I wondered if Rossetti and Burne-Jones, painting their sulky, sexy angels, had for a model someone of Eliana's race, someone who unknown to the painter, or maybe not, had wings?

"The moonlight makes me want to fly," Eliana said.

"I don't blame you. If I'd just gotten wings, I'd want to take them for a spin." I smiled, gave her a playful shove. "Go on. Try your wings." At the same time, I felt a twinge of jealousy. Already her heritage of magic was separating us. This time it would only be for a few hours, but who could say how long it would be before Eliana tired of my dull mortal company?

Then I chuckled at myself for worrying about the future when what we had already shared was beyond all my dreams. "Try your wings," I repeated, really meaning it this time. "I'll be here when you get back."

She cupped my breasts. Nerve endings I thought too sated to respond proved me wrong. "No," she whispered in my ear, "I want us to fly together." Her tongue followed her voice and for a few seconds I could only interpret her suggestion in erotic terms. When it finally sank in, I couldn't do anything but laugh and gesture helplessly with my ordinary human arms.

"It's all right. I'll carry you." I was about to protest that she couldn't possibly, that I weighed more than she did, that it would change her center of gravity, that she needed all her energy to fly. But she sensed my protests and added, "I have my full powers now, remember. I can do things you wouldn't believe." And with these words, she scooped me up like Superman scooping up Lois Lane and took off through the skylight.

Did I mention the skylight wasn't open? (When I asked her later how we did it, all she said was, "Doorknobs and window handles are a convenience for humans. We don't need them.")

It took a while for my heart rate to get back to normal. When I ventured to open my eyes, it leaped up again anyway. We were somewhere well over treetop level, riding a current of air above Eliana's pond. The pond was silver in the moonlight and so was Eliana. The night breeze felt wonderful on my love-sticky skin, and I was bloody petrified. Eliana might be as strong as she said, but her strength was all that came between me and a fatal plunge to earth.

Some semi-detached portion of my mind mocked the irony of it all: here I was, finally having in real life the romantic, fantastic adventure that I'd always sought in literature, with the woman of my dreams, no less, and all I could feel was abject panic. I tried to focus on the night's beauty, on Eliana's closeness, on the miracle of flight. It helped a little, but not much. I noticed, straining to focus on details to calm myself, that she scarcely moved her wings. She rode the air like a hawk riding a thermal.

"I really don't use the wings to fly, except for steering," she said out of nowhere. "I use the magic they embody." I jumped enough that she had to hold me even more tightly. It was going to take a while to get used to her answering my questions before I asked them.

"But you accepted the wings so easily," she said, reading my mind again, "It shouldn't take you long to accept telepathy. In fact, I bet you have some telepathic ability yourself. You're very receptive."

"Only to you," I punned, and kissed her throat, which was what I could reach without moving too much. And suddenly the wild joy of all that had happened flooded me—the soft night air below us, Eliana's silken hair tickling my skin, all the small rustlings and stirrings of a summer night, the love and desire I felt for her. Reading my thoughts again, she bent her head so I could give her a quick kiss.

At least I meant it to be a quick kiss, but Eliana whispered in my blood, something about how magic supported us, that I must have faith, for her powers were the powers of the air. Before I quite knew what had happened, I found myself standing, as it were, on the air, pressed full length against Eliana. I wasn't sure how I'd gotten there, but I felt secure, and her arms were strong around me, and so was her magic, which I could feel holding me up, supporting me, keeping me safe.

"You won't fall," she whispered, her voice sending resonances of excitement even through my bones, which had always been immune to that sort of thing in the past, no matter how much other parts of me were palpitating. "I won't let you fall and neither will the air."

She let go of me.

I screamed, but even as I screamed, I realized I wasn't falling. Although Eliana's arms weren't around me any more, some warm strength supported me. She stroked my hair gently. "You have enough faerie blood," Eliana said, "that my magic works on you, though you don't have the ability yourself. As long as we're touching, you'll fly with me. And believe me, I don't intend for us to stop touching." She put one arm around me again, placed her free hand on my breast. "Relax, Mari," she breathed, and pulled my nipple, hard.

New lovers usually touch each other gently, gingerly. Trust a telepathic faerie, though, to know that I needed something a little harsher to take me past my fear. Nipples stretched and twisted like taffy. Edge of pain blurring quickly to pleasure. I dug my nails into her, moved against her frantically. Teeth at my throat—I would be bruised when this was over. Good.

I put my thigh between her legs, imagined the click as our bodies fitted together. She moved against me, hot juices slicking my skin, and I caught her rhythm and moved with her. She started making small, frantic noises almost immediately, as if there was something especially exciting—and there was—about making love in mid-air. I slipped my hand between us, burrowed just a little into that juicy space, and she cried out so violently that I thought for a second I'd hurt her, until she bit my shoulder and started bucking against me, driving the orgasm to continue. Of course, all this thrashing around had its effect on me, and as I became more and more aroused, Eliana's excitement just seemed to grow.

The rush of night air was cool on my skin and below us the stars were reflecting on Eliana's pond, and the noises we made must have startled the little night creatures for miles, and when I came I felt myself flying on her wings.

And she came again at the same time, her wings beating helplessly against the air, crying out like an animal caught in a trap, a very peculiar sort of trap that it doesn't really want to escape. I smiled that particularly smug grin you smile after you've made your lover explode.

She kept on trembling for a long time. I held her and stroked her back and wings and kissed her eyes and murmured something to the effect of, "It's all right," until she had enough breath back to say, "It's a great deal more than all right!" and we both started nuzzling each other and giggling softly. Around us the cicadas were buzzing. Occasionally a bat flitted past. We were hovering over her pond still. We'd stopped traveling when things got hot, but we'd remained in mid-air.

We kissed once more, deeply and at least on my end somewhat dizzily. Then Eliana asked, "Are you as hot and sticky as I am? No, don't answer. You must be sticky and I know you're hot. Let's go for a swim." Grinning diabolically, she started us down toward the water at what I can only describe as a controlled plummet.

❧ *Stars Inside Her*

I didn't stop screaming until we hit the water. (Actually, I kept on screaming after we hit, because in mid-June in central New York, ponds are cold.) But I was screaming not from fear, but from sheer, giddy joy.

SVYA'S GIRL
Katya Andreevna

Long ago in the Land by the Sea, Maiden lived in a modest dwelling. Although known for her great beauty and vigor, a strange lethargy had overtaken her. She had ceased combing her thick, dark locks. Her clothing had become dirty and ragged, her body weak from inactivity. Most days she sat in her chamber and gazed from the window.

One evening, a sparrow landed on her sill. It hopped and chirped at her excitedly.

"Do be quiet," she said.

But the bird kept up its chatter.

"Am I to accompany you?" she asked the bird. Finally, following the bird's lead, she strolled from her abode. Slowly she moved through the streets, her joints creaking from disuse, her wild hair swarming around her head like a cyclone. Passersby stared at her disheveled state and drew away.

❧ Stars Inside Her

After what seemed like days, Maiden entered a place of great merriment, a tavern she had frequented before the onset of her malaise. As in the past, she waved to the barmaid and passed into the dimly lighted back room.

The room, like always, swirled with energy. By the door, two women were binding a third to a chair. Moans and sighs rose from the crowd gathered around the large table in the middle of the chamber.

"A typical night at The Cave," she thought and sank to the floor in a corner. She blinked her eyes, adjusting to the feeble light. She watched as a powerful woman with silver hair pinned a young woman to the floor. The sliver haired one drew a thick rod from under her garments and with it entered the young woman, who gasped and wrapped her legs around the body above her.

Slumped against the wall, Maiden yawned. "Perhaps I should have bathed," she thought, settling deeper into her torpor. By midnight the passions in the room had reached a boiling point. Women cried out and shook in waves of pleasure. Couples, threesomes, and the group at the table wrestled satisfaction from their bodies in their own way—slaps rang in the air, while the slippery murmurs of lapping tongues created a soothing susurration.

As the ecstasy in the room reached a crescendo, Svya entered. Her appearance was met with intense pleasure. Svya, a renowned traveler, was a favorite in the community. Tall, strong, and commanding, she wore a pair of carefully tailored men's breeches, a hat with a plume, and a richly brocaded vest. A long, jeweled sword hung from the finely tooled belt at her waist.

"Svya, join us," the woman tied to the chair called.

"Svya, where have you been?" another woman asked.

"Out seeking my fortune," Svya replied, striding into the center of the room. Maiden glanced at Svya with a cold eye. She had heard tell of this glorious Svya and in the past she had most desired to meet her.

Svya approached. "Who do we have here?" she asked, leaning down.

Maiden tried to smile. Her wooden cheeks felt as though they would crack from the effort.

Svya snorted with laughter and spun on her heel. She grabbed a passing blonde and, pressing her against the wall, sucked greedily at her breast. Barely breathing, Maiden watched. As her eyes followed Svya, her hands drifted numbly down the flesh of her own cool thighs. But the heavy chill pressed against her, anesthetizing every pore.

Svya made the rounds of the room, massaging breasts, sucking toes, doling out quick spankings. And Maiden watched.

As dawn approached, exhausted women slumped out of the room. Still Maiden lay in her corner, her eyes open, although her body slept. Once again Svya drew near. She smiled down at Maiden."Have you not moved all night?" Svya asked.

Maiden struggled to sit up.

Svya unsheathed her gleaming sword.

Maiden remained perfectly still, but somewhere deep inside, her soul twitched.

Svya drew the flat of the sword up the length of Maiden's leg. Firmly she pushed her legs open, and Maiden offered no resistance. Crouching between

Maiden's legs, Svya parted her fur lips with the hilt of her sword. She pressed the smooth cool handle to Maiden's clit and then pushed inside her.

Maiden lay still.

"Can you feel this?" Svya asked.

Maiden moved her head slowly from side to side. With a sucking noise, Svya withdrew her sword from Maiden's womanhood. She grabbed the still pungent hilt and pressed the sharp point of the blade to Maiden's breast bone.

"Well, can you feel this?" she asked.

The cold steel of the carefully crafted sword, colder than Maiden's cold skin, sliced through her thin blouse. As Maiden inhaled, the slight motion caused the blade to break her skin. A part of Maiden wanted to shove her chest forward onto the steel spike, but her body remained immobile. Maiden took a deep breath and drove the point into the scanty flesh of her sternum.

As Svya drew the tip of the blade down Maiden's chest, the steel flashed cold, then hot. Maiden's breath filled her lungs in short bursts. She tried to speak, but merely gasped as the stinging sword caressed her.

When Svya reached the central point between Maiden's smooth breasts, she withdrew the blade and watched Maiden for a moment. Then sheathing her sword, she cast a handful of gold pieces in Maiden's direction and strode from the chamber.

Maiden looked at the trickle of blood that ran from the wound on her chest.

"Yes," she said as if Svya still stood before her. "Yes, I can feel that." She breathed deeply and her pulse throbbed in her chest, in her wrists, at her temples. A great weight fell away from her body as if she had been cut free from a girdle of thick bark. Like the live green wood below a tree's skin, she tingled with newness. She touched the mark Svya had left on her. Suddenly, like the rising sap, she was flooded with desire.

"Where is Svya?" Maiden demanded.

"I guess she left," one of the few remaining women answered and headed for the door.

Maiden grabbed the woman. Fondling her breasts, Maiden pushed her against the wall. Maiden sucked greedily at the stranger's neck, rubbed against her legs.

"Svya," she thought. "Svya."

Maiden took the money that Svya had thrown. Days and nights she searched for Svya to no avail. She began to travel, searching out craftswomen far and wide. They made for her many a mysterious device dedicated to female pleasure and pain. She tested them all herself, but every new toy merely increased her desire for what she had not felt, the hilt of Svya's sword.

When Maiden came to the Great City, she opened a shop to sell her precious goods, and the fame of her great beauty and strange implements spread through out the land.

One day Svya came to Maiden's shop. Svya gazed long at Maiden's wares. Maiden gazed at Svya, her well muscled legs encased in white breeches, her strong arms, her shining sword.

"Kind Mistress, please explain the use of this implement," Svya asked.

While Maiden explained, choosing her words with care, her heart beat steadily between her legs. She eyed Svya's sword.

"I would be happy to demonstrate the implement," Maiden pronounced finally. Svya smiled and followed Maiden into a private chamber.

"I'll need to warm up a bit," Maiden said. She grabbed Svya's arm and steered her to a chair. Maiden slid the sword at Svya's waist around so that it fell between her new customer's legs. Raising her skirts, Maiden climbed into Svya's lap and lowered herself into the hilt of the much desired sword. The sword was both cold and hot as it had been when it awakened Maiden from her sexless trance. Maiden moved slowly. The weapon was larger than Maiden had remembered. She rocked from side to side as she engulfed the sword, allowing it to caress every inner fold.

Svya stroked Maiden's hair and unbuttoned her blouse. "You are a bold one," Svya whispered into Maiden's ear. "This pleases me."

"I have awaited this a long while," Maiden said, driving the sword deeper inside herself. Maiden rocked on Svya's stiff stem. Her movements became rapid and abrupt. Maiden began to pant. The hot and cold sensation of the sword's steel flooded her whole being. Her body shook in quick spasms and a deep groan crawled from her throat. Maiden drooped against Svya's shoulder for a moment, inhaling deeply. Raising her head she laughed, a full, round, satisfied laugh.

Svya sucked on Maiden's ear lobe. "What is this scar at your breast?" Svya asked, running her thick fingers along the thin slice of white.

Maiden's laughter rang out. She squeezed Svya in her arms and Svya squeezed back. They kissed long and deeply.

After some delay, Maiden replied, "Once I was a prisoner, but a beautiful knight set me free."

Svya stroked Maiden's flushed cheek and Maiden felt herself swimming in the blue pools of Svya's eyes.

"I will tell you the whole story. Some day," Maiden said, removing her blouse and unbuttoning Svya's vest. "Now, I will demonstrate the implement."

SIGHS AND SCREAMS IN FARAWAY TREES

Imat

Shree moved the limb out of the way. Looking from between parted fronds, she felt a sound rise to her throat and she quickly stifled it. She had heard the sound of the villagers raging as they climbed the small hills at the edge of the forest. Thinking it odd that the villagers were making a pilgrimage to the forest at this time of year, she had left her home in the trees to investigate their actions. At first Shree could not hear any of the words being spoken below clearly: the mob was one loud, inaudible, rush of words. Shree listened closely as an ugly, loud voice rose above the noise of the crowd and she heard:

"...You have danced to the music of demons and touched organs with the Horned One, you are a despicable harlot that has brought shame and evil to our village and for this you shall be eaten by the beasts of the forest so that we may be free of your sins!"

Shree had heard these words before; she recognized the voice of the screaming woman now. It was the voice of the preacher's wife, the dirty, hard-eyed witch that Shree could smell even a mile downwind. Shree hated the villagers. It was only with great restraint that Shree kept herself from destroying them.

Shree was surprised to see a young woman standing within the crowd of villagers, her clothes torn and her arms bound behind her. Shree watched as the preacher's wife continued to scream accusations into the helpless woman's face. The young woman did not move, did not flinch, she just stood and stared impassively into the red, bloated face of the woman screaming before her. After a while Shree heard, "Well, Child of the Devil, what say you in your defense?" There was complete silence as the villagers waited to hear the doomed girl's reply.

In a loud, calm voice the young woman replied, "I would rather be eaten by beasts and mauled by demons than willingly accept the touch of your hand, Carlan." Shree smiled at these words. She had never understood why so many young women were thrown into the forests by these stupid villagers, but now it was clear; they had refused the preacher's wife! With her God on her side, Carlan punished their refusals by putting them to death.

Shree had seen many young women cast into the forest to perish at the hands of beasts and demons, but had taken no interest in the fate of their dull and stupid existence. Shree was familiar with the pleading, crying, and begging of women sent into the forest, but she had never seen defiance or indifference in a village woman.

Shree watched as Carlan slapped the young woman hard across the face with her open palm; she watched as the young woman withstood the blow without so much as a sway.

"Cut free her arms and cast her into the forest to be reunited with her lover, the Demon of Darkness," Carlan screeched.

Shree watched as the young woman was brutally thrown into the forest. She heard the curses of the villagers as they began their long journey back to the village; watched as they ran to escape the sun that was beginning to set. Who was this strange village girl that had dared to defy the powerful and ugly Carlan?

The setting sun lit the forest canopy in splashes of orange light, casting spotted, irregular markings on the figure of the young girl walking barefoot on the moss-covered forest floor below. The young woman, bathed in the fire and light of the setting sun evoked memories of legends Shree had been told as a child. Her mother had told stories of a mythical creature that was half-human and half-snow leopard, the guardian of all that was female and sacred in the forest. No one ever saw this Goddess without being transformed by her grace and power. Shree was not sure if her hunger and the waning sun were playing tricks on her eyes, but the young woman below seemed to shape shift as she walked. Shree decided to wait and watch her a little longer before taking her.

When the girl came to an open space within the forest, she stopped walking. She stood bathed in the fading orange light, raised her arms above her head, lifted her face to the sky and yelled in a surprisingly strong voice,

"I am La'Dess, child of the Harvest Fires. I am hungry and alone in this forest. Hear me spirits of the trees, for I am."

La'Dess moved her arms slowly, in complicated patterns and circles, moving her body to a rhythm beating deep within her. Watching La'Dess, Shree could feel the internal rhythm that the girl danced to. The girl removed her dirty rags and danced with them clenched in her hands, held above her head as if she were offering them as a gift, or perhaps a challenge, to the gods.

In her lifetime Shree had stalked many creatures in the forest; she had enjoyed eating the flesh of many and had even enjoyed just tasting some of them and letting them go. Shree knew that in just a few broad steps she could capture this young woman, take her down on the moist forest floor with little effort. Shree wanted this woman, but remained still and captivated by her private dance.

Shree watched as the girl dropped her clothes upon the ground, placed one hand behind her back, threw her head back, and ran her fingers slowly across her neck. Palm open, nails pressed deep into the flesh, back and forth she ran her fingers across her throat as she danced. Shree thought she heard the sound of a low growl, but she was not sure if the sound came from her own throat or that of the girl's. Shree watched as the girl openly offered herself to the gods of the forests. Rage and contempt stirred within her, how dare the gods ignore the offering of this young woman?

La'Dess turned slowly in circular movements, one arm still placed behind her back, her legs parted the width of two hands as she swayed to her own rhythm, stroking her throat as if she were in a trance. La'Dess' dance ended and she dropped slowly to her knees, parted them wide, her back arched, her head almost touching the ground. Her arms forming an arch joined behind her back, she became still as if suspended in time.

Shree stared at the stretched and open body of La'Dess, watched as her large, round nipples disappeared into themselves, forming solid, protruding nipples that appeared to be pulled by invisible mouths above them. The sweet, unexpected flash of pink flesh that was open and visible from between parted thighs made Shree bite her own lip until she tasted blood, intensifying her hunger. Shree imagined she could smell the scent of La'Dess from where she perched above her.

The sight and smell of the young woman stretched out below her was overwhelming Shree. Her mind raged when she thought of the indifference of the bodiless gods of the forests ignoring the perfect gift of flesh and blood that this young woman offered. "I will take what the gods have no use for and to hell with their wrath," she growled deeply.

With her decision made, Shree swiftly descended from her hiding place in the forest trees and stood before the soft and open young woman. La'Dess was startled by the presence of Shree and she tried to stand, but the awkwardness of her position made her movements slow. Shree said in a low voice, "Do not move, you shall remain as you have offered yourself." Shree could smell the woman's fright, and it stirred her hunger. Shree roughly grabbed La'Dess' breast in her hands, filling her hands with the full softness of her skin as she pulled and pinched the nipples roughly. The sensation of taking this woman burned through Shree's blood and when La'Dess cried out and tried to cover herself, Shree growled, "Do not try to cover yourself or I shall tie you." La'Dess made a small sound of protest, but stopped moving. Shree went down on her knees before the trembling young woman she had waited so long to taste. Shree breathed deeply, filling herself with the scent of tender, young flesh. Shree lowered her head and opened the young woman's soft lips. She wanted to see how deep the pinkness ran before she sank her mouth into the sweet cunt she held in her hands.

The forest seemed to be alive with invisible flames in the silent darkness, lit now only by the witnessing moon. La'Dess had begun her death dance by slipping deep into herself, dancing to her heartbeat as memories poured from her soul. She had surrendered herself to the forest of her own free will rather than accept the touch of the woman who had broken the backs of many young women in the village with her secret and endless jealous perversion. Carlan. She had felt the woman's eye on her since she was a child, she knew one day she would have to make a choice and she did not regret the one she had made. Death at the hands of demons was preferable to life in the hands of a woman who did evil while hiding behind the protection of a righteous god. La'Dess did not regret her choice, as she waited for the forest to accept her life. Time passed slowly, as if each moment were hewn from stone.

When La'Dess had opened her eyes and saw the large woman with wild eyes before her, she thought that death had come to claim her. She had not expected to see the instrument of her demise and when she saw it in the form of a woman she had risen to meet her fate. The woman's strength seemed immeasurable, unreal, she could not break free of her hands that seemed to be all over her exposed body at once. When the woman commanded her to be still or be tied, she chose to be still rather than die bound. La'Dess could feel the hot, rapid breath on her vulnerable and trembling clit and she wondered if she would be eaten alive or if the woman would kill her first. La'Dess did not struggle, it made no difference to her. Her fate had been decided and she knew that she was to die in this forest, naked and with no witness of her own kind; it did not matter how it came to pass, at the hands of woman, man, beast, or demon.

La'Dess felt the breath upon her cunt grow hotter and quicker and she steeled herself for the anticipated pain. When the mouth began to devour her she nearly fainted, suspended between fear, pain and pleasure. La'Dess surrendered herself to the intensity of the sensations coursing through her body and lost consciousness.

The forest floor was moist and cool beneath her burning flesh as she began to stir from the strange darkness that had consumed her consciousness. When she opened her eyes she expected to find a world of fire and flame, but instead was surprised by a deeply tanned woman's face staring intently into her own just a few inches from her. La'Dess could feel the pressure of the large woman's body pressing down upon her and she was certain her body would be crushed beneath the weight of the powerful woman. Anticipating the sound of a witch's laughter, waiting for the pain of a knife blade to pierce her soft skin, she closed her eyes again. The sky did not break open in a thunderous roar, her heart was not ripped from her body, no knife slipped into her soft belly. She felt the woman's large and callused hands on her shoulders, felt the sensation as the woman pressed her muscular body harder into her soft skin; she was certain she would be crushed, her bones cracked and broken, but instead the woman pulled her to a standing position. Before she could orient herself to the feel of the ground beneath her feet, the woman let her fall abruptly from her grasp, catching her before she fell to the ground. She held her body with one arm, and grabbed her hair with her other hand and thrust her head back so that they were staring into one another's eyes, the woman held her gaze and said in a voice that seemed not quite human, "I claim you, you are mine."

La'Dess stood her ground where the woman placed her, watching as she circled her again and again. She felt as if she were getting smaller with each circle the woman made. The sound that came from the circling woman reminded La'Dess of the big cats that attacked her family's sheep in the mountains where she had grown up. La'Dess remembered the fear and awe that had possessed her as she watched the sheep fall one by one to the big cats, horrified by what she saw but unable to look away from what she was powerless to stop. Her heart had gone out to her sheep, her nightmares filled with the anguish of wondering how they had felt right before their throats were ripped open by the massive creatures that sprang endlessly from the dark night. La'Dess remembered that night clearly now as she waited for the woman to tear into her body with savage ferocity. The woman grabbed her from behind, pressing into her ass, with one arm around her waist, the other pulling mercilessly on one of her breasts as she pushed, pulled and thrust herself into La'Dess with a strength that defied her mortal form. Her body absorbed the assault that seemed to strike every nerve, her cries seemed to inspire the woman to increase the force of her thrusting as she pulled harder on La'Dess' breasts.

La'Dess felt as if her blood had been set to flame, her mind melted into the sensation of being devoured alive. Her legs burned and she felt weak as the woman put her hand on the back of her neck and forced her to bend over until her hands touched the ground. La'Dess felt the air rush around her burning body as the woman stepped away from her, she could still feel the heat of the woman's breath on her ass, she could feel the large hands on her legs and thighs as they paused for a moment before she thrust one hand between La'Dess' legs and opened her lips wide, holding the warm, plump flesh open to the night air. In one swift moment, the world was turned upside down as the woman grabbed her ankles and lifted her upside down in the air. La'Dess saw the ground below her as the woman lifted her body further and further into the air as she hung upside down, her feet pointing towards the sky, her arms struggled to touch the ground she could not reach. The woman held her tightly as she bit her thighs until she had no choice but to part them, her legs folded across the strong shoulders of the woman who sank her mouth into her open cunt. La'Dess could feel the sharp teeth, the hard, long tongue that forced itself deep inside her as the woman bit and sucked her with a wildness that reduced her to screams. She pressed her face into the woman's hard stomach, while the blood rushed to her head and her mind exploded from the sensations every nerve in her body fired. She felt as if she were spinning in endless time as the woman held her tightly while she turned in circles, growling into her soft flesh as she devoured her completely. The world faded away into nothing but explosions of color and pleasure, she felt her body being turned and folded into itself over and over until it no longer belonged to her. When the woman laid her down on the forest floor she felt as if it rose up to her, took her into its arms and embraced her, she let her mind follow her body into the gentle cool earth that soothed her bruised and burning body. She no longer knew where her body left off and the forest began.

When she regained consciousness she felt the pain in her body and she began to cry when she realized she was still alive. She had thought she had finally found a way out of the body that had always betrayed her, she longed for the feeling of being pulled into the mouth of a demon again. The sweat on her young body began to chill her and she became aware of her nakedness. She tried to cover her breasts with her hands but she heard a strong voice command, "Open your thighs for me."

La'Dess whimpered, "I cannot."

A great roar was heard in the forest as the woman leapt upon her again, grabbing her hair with one hand, she held her tightly and kissed her roughly, consuming La'Dess' screams with her hungry kiss. La'Dess could not breathe. Her body was alive, her cunt swollen and throbbing as if it had grown a new heart of its own where the woman had devoured her not long before. Never had

La'Dess felt so exposed and defenseless, as if her skin had been peeled away and her nerves exposed to the sensations of the world. Just as La'Dess was feeling faint again from lack of air, the woman took away her mouth. La'Dess opened her eyes and as she did so she saw a flash of silver in the woman's hand and she thought, "Ah, the knife, it comes at last," and she closed her eyes. The woman slapped her hard across the face with her open palm. She opened her eyes, looked into the wild, intense eyes that held her stare with a ferocity that stirred her soul. The woman moved the knife along La'Dess face, slowly moving the leather handle across her lips as she said,

"This is the knife of my mother, the knife whose handle she plunged into a sleeping queen, stealing the seed of a king and slipping it into herself. I am the child of the stolen seed of a king, whose queen sucked at my mother's breasts, while her husband, the king, sent knights on horseback into the forest to search for her. My mother won a queen with the handle of this knife, she deceived and robbed a king with the handle of this knife, and I shall take you and defy fate with this knife, and your blood shall cement the bond."

La'Dess shook in horror as she felt the smooth leather handle of the knife tracing, stroking, and caressing the insides of her thighs. True! All true! La'Dess remembered the stories her grandmother had told of the Vampiress that lived in the forest, capturing and devouring victims. Grandmother had said that the Vampiress was no child of man! La'Dess felt Shree's mouth on her breast, pulling and biting her nipple so hard that her whole body felt as if it were burning. She could feel

Shree's hand clenched tightly around the back of her neck, fear and sensation keeping her paralyzed. La'Dess felt the knife handle as it was forced into her, she felt the pain of penetration and the warmth of blood slipping into her buttocks, as Shree moved the knife she clenched in her fist into La'Dess. La'Dess felt her muscles tighten around the knife handle, felt her body move into it, wanting it as Shree pushed it deeper and with more intensity. La'Dess felt as if she were melting into Shree's hand and she gasped as she felt Shree's mouth sucking her rigid, swollen clit while she still plunged the knife handle into her deeply and slowly. She began to scream as she lost herself to a new madness that spread throughout her body.

Screaming, La'Dess looked about the forest in the moon's light, searching for a way out of this body that betrayed her. She saw the women's faces staring out from the massive trees and remembered what her mother had told her, "I found you in the trees and they whispered your name to me. I do not believe you were born of woman but of the forest itself." She had never understood what this meant until she looked now, at the trees surrounding her, witnessing her death. She had come home at last and she surrendered herself to the hunger of the woman the forest had also bred.

There was no sound in the forest, not even the wind stirred the tree tops towering above. The moon paled itself as a woman sat alone in the darkness. As Shree looked down upon the woman who lay silently at her feet, she was overcome with sadness and her anguished

cry rang throughout the still forest. She had killed the gift
of the gods by wanting too much. But Shree's cry stirred
La'Dess, who woke to find soft green eyes staring into
her own, a single tear ran down a darkly tanned cheek. A
tear! La'Dess knew that vampires were unable to cry.
La'Dess stared at Shree who had the knife still in her
hand, the handle stained dark with the blood and moisture of her body. Shree was looking at La'Dess but she
could not see her through her tears, she believed the
woman to be dead. Shree stood to leave, turned back to
look one last time at the gift her hunger had destroyed,
and she saw the woman move her arm. She was not dead
after all! Shame and awe consumed her, it did not seem
possible that a mortal woman had withstood the drive of
her desire and the violence of her lust.

Shree was filled with sadness and the certainty that
the promise she had made to her mother would have to
be honored. Shree either would be accepted by the
woman she had claimed and taken by force or, if rejected, take her life for the crime of her theft. Shree knelt
down beside La'Dess and lay the knife gently between her
young breasts, saying, "You are free to go, stay or kill me
for that which I have taken from you, or you may give
yourself to me and I shall die defending and devouring
you."

La'Dess looked into the face of the woman who
knelt before her. Go? Where could she go? Home to the
villagers who had sacrificed her? Her home and chosen
family had long since been destroyed by the fires of the
one-god soldiers. There was no home to return to. Should
she kill this woman for waking her spirit and flesh when
she had offered herself to death? La'Dess imagined

spending her life being devoured and protected by a woman made by no man and bound to none. La'Dess placed her hand on the blade of the knife laying between her breasts, staring Shree in the eyes as she rose shakily to her feet. Shree felt shame for her crime of wanting, for her theft of La'Dess, and she prepared to die for her crime, closing her eyes and breathing deeply as she waited for the knife to strike.

Shree gasped as she felt the sharp pain of her mother's knife handle penetrate into her body where nothing but her own hand had ever been. Shree opened her eyes and looked into the cool green eyes of La'Dess as she heard her say, "I claim you, you are mine."

As the sun rose in the forest at the edge of the waterfalls, two women lay wrapped in each other's arms, each with bloodied hands and stained thighs, happier than anyone ever lets women outside of forests at the edge of waterfalls ever be.

LILITH
Jessy Luanni Wolf

The first time Lilith came to me I thought she was a ghost. I was dreaming a terrible dream about being devoured alive by a horrible monster. Lost in my dream-scape, I struggled to escape from something huge, amorphous, darkly multicolored and with teeth that gleamed in the night. I stumbled across sand, my body unresponsive to the adrenaline pumping flight messages of "faster, faster!" through my veins. I wanted to wake up but my eyes wouldn't open, my limbs wouldn't move. I knew I was asleep, I knew I was in a dream. I tried to fly, I reached up to catch the wind, as the monster gained on me and drew closer. I pulled myself up, I was so heavy, the air felt so thick, I had to push up through it to fly towards the sky. I pulled myself up, and at the same time tried desperately to open my eyes. Finally, slowly, I awakened. My eyes opened to the midnight darkness of my room as I pushed through the heavy mud of sleep. I forced my consciousness back into my body and felt my limbs come alive so that I could move one finger, then another. My breath squeezed painfully from my lungs and my heart thundered in my chest as I made my escape from something too awful to exist in reality. Suddenly, I realized that my whole bed was shaking. At first, I thought the bed was merely an extension of my trembling body. But my trembling faded as I gained consciousness and the bed—the bed was still shaking. I thought, is this an earthquake? I looked around the dark room and saw the shadows of my things. All were still and calm in their places. The bed continued to shake and I knew that an earthquake would have ended several minutes ago. My heart started to pound again as I realized the shaking bed had to be caused by a ghost.

I believe in ghosts. I believe in angels, in demons, in gods and goddesses, in fairies and elves. So I had no trouble accepting that a ghost might choose to haunt me.

"What do you want, ghost?" I whispered in the darkness. I heard a soft chuckle and just for a second, my heart stopped. I added, "Who are you, what do you need from me?"

"I am not a ghost." The voice was musical and low; a woman's voice. I felt the soft touch of a kiss on my lips. Then she added, "I am Lilith."

"Lilith! As in Adam's first wife?" I asked.

"I am the first woman," she stated proudly. She, unlike Eve, was formed from the dust the same way as Adam and so had an equal status. Adam complained that she wanted to be on top during sex, and tried to force her to stay on the bottom, while Lilith complained that Adam was an inferior lover and couldn't satisfy her. She finally used the magic word of God's true name to escape from Eden. Adam's second wife, Eve, was created to be much more docile.

"Lilith, in case you hadn't noticed, I'm a woman," I told her. Again, I heard her melodious laughter flow into the darkness and swirl all around me. I felt the touch of a finger stroking my nipple. A delightful shiver ran up and down my spine. I felt the pressure of her lips as she kissed me and I kissed her back. I strained in the darkness to see her, but I saw nobody.

"I have always liked women best," she said. "I only use men so I can make my babies." She kissed me again. I felt her tongue dart in between my teeth to taste my own tongue. I felt her hands squeeze my breasts. A delicious thrill ran through my body.

"Where are you? I can't see you!" I managed to gasp out between the moans of pleasure her hands and tongue were eliciting from me. I could feel her firm body pressed against mine. Her hair tickled my skin as she kissed my neck and face. But I couldn't see anything at all, she was invisible. I brought my arms up to stroke her back, which I found by touch alone. Her skin was silky smooth. She seemed to have mountains of hair, thick and heavy. I wove my fingers into her hair which curled into long ringlets that fell all around us. I'd never felt hair like hers, which felt so strong and curled so tightly into thick ropes. I wanted to see them, to fit what I felt into some reality I could identify. Then, the pleasure my body felt in response to Lilith took over my brain and I left the reasoning human behind as I became purely an animal of sensations.

Lilith was an artist, she played my body as if I were a great work of art in progress. My nipples hummed, my

91

lips swelled, my inner thighs burned, my buttocks stung and my vagina throbbed with something beyond pleasure or pain. I could feel but not see, and I could only lie there and feel one rush of feeling after another. Pain and pleasure sometimes separated into distinct feelings and then blended into one mixed sensation that was neither but somehow transcended both. *Lilith!* I called her name several times, begged her to let me see what she was doing, to let me see her. I wanted to touch her, to love her back, but she always moved away from my embrace and I never could quite grasp her. And all the time, she hummed, she sang words in some ancient language I couldn't recognize, and she laughed her deep rich laugh whenever I tried and failed to hold her. I strained in the night to see her. I felt my body rise up to meet an orgasm and then always, over and over, Lilith gave me a sharp pain which chased the orgasm away. I was strung so tightly that my nerves felt like fine wire stretched taut. My breasts ached, they felt bruised and sore. My belly was yearning for fulfilment and my vulva was swollen in anticipation of a release that never seemed to come.

Lilith laughed. "I have you just where I want you," she said. I felt her move her body up along mine, rubbing herself against me as she moved upwards. I felt her breasts rise up along my chest and neck and stop when my lips touched her nipple.

"Suck!" she commanded me. "But be gentle," she added.

I licked her nipple and pulled it into my mouth with my tongue. I rolled her tight little point of a nipple all around my tongue and gently, so gently, sucked on it. I heard her moan in pleasure. I nibbled softly on the tip with my teeth, and she gasped. Then I noticed that I could just barely see her silhouette. She held her head back, arching her back. The long ropes of hair fell all around her. She pulled her nipple from my mouth and pulled her body upwards, so that I felt her curly, tickly pubic hair as it slid up my belly, chest and neck, and landed right on my mouth. I slid my tongue between the hair and found the soft, moist, secret places hidden within. My heart beat faster with all the frustrated desire I still had, held at the peak and waiting to explode. I stroked her with my tongue, sucked her button when I found it, and bit all around it as I sucked and stroked her with my tongue. My own body ached to feel what she was feeling. I watched her silhouette writhe as she moaned and gasped in time to my lips and tongue. She grew gradually more solid as she came closer and closer to her peak. My body screamed in jealous frustration as I felt her come and I saw her body materialize completely during the shudders of her orgasm.

She was dark—so dark, except the inner part of her vulva which was still right above my face. That was a delicious shade of pink. The ropes of hair I'd felt I now saw were dreadlocks. Lilith was Black.

"I thought you were Jewish!" I told her, for a moment so surprised that my frustrated body receded from my mind.

"The Jews have been through many changes since the beginning," she said, "and you know even your modern scientists now admit that Africa is the cradle of humanity. I am the first woman, so naturally I am African, as was Adam, as was Eve."

She was beautiful, strong, proud, and she was still on top of me. I smelled the rich musky scent of her and felt the familiar throb begin again in my loins.

"Oh, Lilith, don't leave me like this, please finish me," I begged her.

She laughed at me. "Too bad for you, girl," she said, as she climbed off of my bed and stood facing me. "I'm done." She smiled at me. "But I think I'd like to watch you give yourself the pleasure you wanted from me."

I felt myself flush. I had never done anything like that in front of another person. "I can't do it," I said. My body ached and throbbed, wanting release.

"Do it," she commanded. She leaned back against the wall opposite my bed, watching me. She smiled a slow, lazy smile. "I want to watch you come," she said. "I will even tell you what to do." She pointed at me and continued, "Pinch your nipples."

Slowly I brought my hands up to my breasts, and pinched my own nipples. It felt very good, but my whole body flushed in shame because she was watching me.

"Good," she said, "now squeeze your breasts and rub your nipples for a while."

I squeezed and then rubbed, squeezed and rubbed. My body heated up and though I continued to feel shamed by her gaze, I also responded to the actions of my own hands.

"Okay, that's nice," she said. "Spread open your legs so I can look at you."

I opened my legs and felt the cool night air touch my innermost tender parts. Lilith stood opposite me, smiling. She rubbed her belly in a circular movement, slowly.

"Stroke yourself," she commanded.

I flushed hotly, I felt a keen mixture of heat, pleasure, and shame as I slowly began to rub my vulva. As my fingers moved over my clitoris I felt a sharp stab of pleasure shoot from my touch all the way up to the base of my skull. It was so delicious. I looked at Lilith. She was smiling, and stroking her own genitals as she watched me. I moaned and continued to rub and squeeze and stroke my own throbbing center of pleasure with one hand as I squeezed the nipple of my breast with the other. Suddenly, I felt a whip strike me on my thighs, with stinging pain. A welt rose across my tender skin as I cried out. I looked to Lilith, but she was still standing there, smiling and stroking herself. I saw no whip, but then I felt it again, across my breasts, and I heard it snap. Just for a second I thought I saw a creature hovering above me. Wings, a long slinky tail, and another snap as the tail struck me across my tender breasts one more time. I heard Lilith chuckle.

"Turn over," she said. I obeyed, knowing what was to follow. A little thrill of anticipation traveled up my spine, half of fear, half of pleasure. I slid my hand under my belly so I could continue pleasuring myself, and just as my fingers found my silky pubic hair, I felt the sharp snap of the creature's whipping tail across my bare buttocks. I cried out with the intense pain I felt when the whip stung my soft flesh. Then I found the spot my fingers sought and gave myself the pleasure I wanted so badly. Snap! The whip came down again, and Lilith laughed. I allowed my imagination only a moment to wonder just who or what was whipping me before I became lost in the mixture of pain and pleasure my nerves were immersed in. My buttocks reddened with the quick succession of snap snap snap from the creature's tail. My heart raced, my breath stopped and then panted furiously as each touch of the tail first caught me and then held me in the passion of pain. Gradually the mix of pleasure and pain began to peak, pulling me higher and higher up a rugged mountain of alternating sensations, punctuated with Lilith's laughter. Just as I knew I could bear no more, that I must rush over the peak and either come or die, Lilith stopped me. I felt her hands on me, pushing me over onto my back again, pulling my hands away from my body. I fought her, I screamed at her, I begged her to let me finish—but she only laughed.

"I have a friend," Lilith said. "I want you to pleasure my friend."

"No!" I shook my head. "I just want you, Lilith."

"You've got no choice," she said, "and anyway, my friend has been here the whole time. My pet has let you feel the power of her tail. She tells me it has made her very happy. But now she needs something more. You won't see her, but right about now you should feel her!"

I felt something very hot—almost too hot to bear, touch me. Then, I felt strong fingers with sharp claws grasp my breasts and knead them as if they were two lumps of dough being turned into bread. It hurt—my breasts hurt, my insides hurt, she was so hot, so rough. She filled up my belly and I felt stretched to my limit. Suddenly, she pulled away and then I felt something inserted into my rectum, hot, big, it was too much for me, I screamed. I felt at that moment something hot shoot upwards into my body, burning me as it flowed up through my intestines. I heard a gruff voice purring and for a second, a shape flickered into reality and out again, and I saw something red and gold, with wings and haunches shaped like a cat, a long tail, the head was feathered but had fangs like a lion and eyes like a woman.... no, my brain rejected it, I couldn't accept the reality of the thing I saw.

Lilith laughed. Then she came over to me, and very softly, she began to lick my engorged little center cf pleasure. All my muscles relaxed with the acceptance cf pleasure. Lilith sucked gently and sent shivers of electricity racing across my belly and buttocks. I felt the tightness spreading from the point of pleasure caressed by Lilith's tongue and up my spine which signaled the rush of sensations about to burst free. Lilith removed her mouth from my body and I moaned in protest, thinking she was about to deny me release. She laughed softly and kissed my vulva before she licked my juices in an upward stroke which ended right on the center of all sensations. Then she brought me over the edge with a soft little bite and a very gentle suck. My entire being felt blissfully happy. I snuggled down into my bed, exhausted and satisfied, and as I fell asleep I heard Lilith say, "I'll be seeing you later."

In the morning I decided the whole thing had just been a really strange dream. I went on about my life, went to work, to the store, to see friends, and tried to forget about Lilith. I was a teacher, I taught English at the local Community College. For awhile I was able to immerse myself in the reading, lecturing and correcting papers required by my job.

One day, I was in front of a Freshman English class describing the process of revision. This particular class had been reluctant to rewrite papers and as a result I read many essays in need of both editing and revision. So, I lectured about the writing process and an assignment with revision built into it, along with peer collaboration. The class was unresponsive; I could see they did not want to do this, so I stepped up my tone and tried to generate enthusiasm.

Suddenly, I heard Lilith's low laugh. She was there, next to me. She said, "Don't worry, nobody sees or hears me but you."

I looked at the class, and they did seem just as poker-faced as before. I felt Lilith behind me, she pressed against me and brought her arms around my body and squeezed my breasts.

"Careful," she said, "you mustn't let the class know I'm here. Just keep on with your lecture while I enjoy myself." She pinched my nipples and bit my neck as she pressed her body into mine.

What could I do? I continued to lecture as best as I could, while Lilith played with my body. I discovered that she could slide right under my clothes, and not show a hint that she was there. But I could feel her. I felt her bite my nipples, stroke my belly, insert her tongue into all my various orifices, and lick my most tender and sensitive spots. I tried very hard to talk about revision and collaboration all the while throbbing with pain and pleasure. Finally I gave them an essay assignment to start writing in class. Then I just stood there, as Lilith flooded my body with sensations. I watched the clock, and just as the time came to release the class, my body thundered to a tremendous orgasm which I tried very hard to conceal from the exiting students.

One boy lingered and asked, "Is this essay due tomorrow?"

I just managed to answer him with a nod of my head, as wave after wave of pleasure washed over me. I heard Lilith's laughter fading away as I gathered my things up to leave. "See you soon," she whispered.

For the next week Lilith came to me every night and aroused me just to the point of orgasm and left me there, unfinished. I was worn pretty thin and was willing to do anything she wanted just to get the release my body craved. Even so, I continued to work as usual, and on Friday I had to go out of town to a conference required by my job. I drove to the conference, which was in a city two hours away from my home. I checked in to the conference and wandered among the exhibits, gathering information on new textbooks and other products. Then it was time for the keynote speaker to begin the address. I found a seat near the back and settled in. The chair was cool, and I squirmed a bit, trying to get some small relief from the aching horniness I felt. Suddenly, Lilith was there, kissing me. I felt the little friend watching, and knew the time had come—she wanted me to satisfy the Gryphon. I wondered why Lilith always brought the Gryphon and wanted me to satisfy her. I heard Lilith answer in my mind.

"She has been with me since I escaped from Adam and took demon lovers. She is my favorite, she gives me the most pleasure, so she is always with me." Lilith kissed my breasts and sucked on my nipples. The little friend was next to my face, I felt her heat. A man, a stranger, came and sat on my left, where the little friend was. The little friend flickered into reality for a moment and I saw she was sitting on the man's shoulder, grinning at me and stroking her feathers as her long tail slithered all around her. The man didn't see the Gryphon. Two ladies sat on my right, talking about the pay schedule of their school district. I saw Lilith pinch them on their breasts and grin as each in turn looked startled. Then she turned to me. I saw her perfectly clearly, and I felt uneasy because she was so visible to me I thought others must have known she was there. But nobody seemed to notice.

She reached right through my clothes to stroke my breasts, my belly, and my vulva. I tingled in anticipation. But she stopped. She kissed my face, and whispered in my ear, "First take care of my little friend." I sighed, and involuntarily my muscles tightened against the pain to come. She was always so hot, so rough—she hurt so much—so I tensed, waiting. "You must spread your legs wide," Lilith said. I looked to my side at the man. Would he notice? He was right next to me; and the ladies, they were gossiping now but suppose they glanced at me, wouldn't they wonder why I sat with my legs apart? What if I made some sort of sound? I would have to be totally silent no matter what. Suddenly, against my lips, I felt the Gryphon's hot tongue.

"Kiss her," Lilith commanded. How could I? I hated the very thought of it! And also, my face, it would show, and what would these people think if they saw me kissing at the air with my legs open? Lilith laughed. "Kiss her!" She commanded again. I felt her hand reach down between my legs and start to stroke me gently. I opened my mouth, and felt the hot scaly tongue enter and twine around my own tongue. I felt my lips spread as I tried to escape the heat of the Gryphon's tongue, and I started to kiss, moving my own tongue in a lover's dance with the tongue of the Gryphon. I was careful not to make a sound, even when she started to move her tongue faster in my mouth, choking me at times, rubbing my lips raw with the heat and the scales. I tasted my own blood as her roughness scraped my tongue raw. Suddenly she was inside my vagina, pumping furiously as she squeezed and scratched and pinched my poor nipples, and whipped me on my back and sides with her stinging tail. I felt her feathered head brush my cheek and then I felt the pain as she bit into my tender neck with her lion's fangs. And then, with the pain, I felt intense pleasure and shame that I could feel this way. Lilith all the while, laughed. I saw her move to the man next to me and stroke his penis. He quickly covered his lap with his hands, trying to hide his erection. She laughed again and moved her face right through his hands so she could suck out his sperm as he came. She looked at me.

"For my babies," she said, "I have to make more than are destroyed each day as my punishment for refusing to return to Adam." The Gryphon was still pumping, pushing my legs further and further apart. She was getting hotter and hotter, I felt my body blistering from the heat. She clawed my breasts savagely, and bit me again on the neck as she came, shooting red hot fire into my body, burning all the way into my womb—hot, so hot, I felt a mixture of pleasure and pain so strong that I needed to scream but I couldn't, I had to be silent. The man next to me was slumped in his chair, covering his lap, looking straight ahead. He had no idea what had happened to him, or why. Lilith was again pinching the nipples of the two ladies on my other side, distracting them. She stroked the vulva of first one, then the other, and whispered erotic messages to their subconscious minds. She told me, "I am the one who subverts women away from the rule of men."

I wanted to ask her for details, ask what she meant, but there were people all around, the entire room was full of people, I had to be silent, and this time she did not answer my thoughts. The Gryphon lifted from me and flew up to hover above us. Lilith came to me. She kissed me softly on the lips, and gently stroked my breasts. "Mine," she said, "you are all mine and always will be." Then she moved to the floor, and brought her face to between my thighs. My whole body sighed in anticipation, and I quivered as I felt her tongue touch me softly and start to stroke, so gently, so softly, bringing me up and up and up to the highest point and then, just as I peaked, she bit me hard right on the tip of my clitoris, and sucked it hard, pulling a thudding, booming, earth-shaking orgasm from me which I had to enjoy in complete silence, without moving a muscle. Again she whispered to me, "You are mine—and no man shall ever satisfy you again." Then she was gone.

I never discovered what the Keynote Speaker had said. I never spoke to any of the people who had sat next to me. I went through the rest of the conference dazed, bruised and sore, wanting only to get home, take a shower, and look for the evidence on my body of what I'd been through.

And I wondered, why did Lilith pick me?

And I wondered, will she come again?

Part of me hoped she never would return, that she would leave me in peace to live my life in a normal way.

But the other part, the secret part, was terrified at the thought that she might never return. That hidden part of me longed intensely for the next moment her soft laughter would enter my head and her touch thrill my soul. I belonged to Lilith, as she'd said, I was hers. But what did she mean? No man would ever satisfy me again—I knew that. Still; as I waited for Lilith to return to me, I felt my body yearn to feel the touch of hands beside my own. I found my eyes watching women on the street, and wondering, what would they taste like, how would their bodies feel next to mine? As I imagined kissing a woman I saw on the street, I seemed to hear Lilith's soft laughter. Then I knew, Lilith might never return to me but I could still feel the kind of pleasure she had made me realize I needed. As I passed by a colorful little bookstore I'd always known was there, I turned and went through the door. On the floor, I saw stacks of free periodicals. One was called *The Lesbian News*. I picked it up and carried it home. I knew that somewhere within those pages, I would find just what I was looking for. In the reflection of the storefront window, for just a minute, I saw Lilith smile.

THE GATE OF DEAD BIRDS
Jana McCall

Only fools like me seek out the underside of the Gate of the Dead Birds. There is little reason to use it at the north side of the Academy campus, not when the main road runs by the South Gate. Its dark grey stone and wide oak beam construction combine to present an intimidating facade. And for the last few years something has lurked in the immenseness of its rafters, preying on the winged things that try to perch there and feeding on their small souls.

The corpses tumble to the floor and take forever to stop twitching. And those few of us insane enough to walk among them almost never dare to look up.

Once, when I was more innocent, I loved the "something." Or at least I loved the "someone" who became the "something." Even now, when I am a little older and a lot battered by what has happened, I still maintain the illusion that what I feel might be the thread Maggie can follow back.

So I walk under the Gate, picking my way among the masses of blood and feathers.

"Carla!" A familiar voice cascades down from the heights. Her use of my name tempts me to glance up.

I trace the four-pointed sign over my lips, warding them and reminding myself to be careful. "I'm here," I answer.

"Look at me, love. Carla, sweetheart, just look at me." Her voice hasn't changed. It still resounds with husky promises and secret laughter.

"No, Maggie." Bad enough that my body betrays me, that I still feel her phantom touch on my breasts, on my stomach, on my legs. I will not let myself be deceived by the sight of her.

"Look at me, Carla," she begs.

I focus instead on the dead birds, glinting in the few stray shafts of sunlight. They are real, all too real, and they will not bespell me. "No."

Her voice edges toward anger as it always does. "Then go away. You're good at that. Go back to your precious mage-masters and their sacred texts and their rules."

I wish I could. But there is a barrier between me and the Mysteries—and its source is here. Until I break through, I'm drawn back again and again to this place and my once lover in the rafters.

"Go away!" She shrieks the words at me, like a crow preparing to attack. I stand my ground. By the sentence of the Most Senior Sage, she is restricted to the boundaries of the sanctuary, and cannot harm those who stand on its ground. I dig the toes of my black boots into the dust and draw strength from the earth.

A quick flutter of wings and a streak of grey and red herald the presence of a foolish bird trying to fly under the gate. I do not need to hear Maggie's chuckle to know she has caught it. Six spatters of blood fall around me in a circle. I wait. It is hard to tell whether the shrieks from above are pain or glee.

"I wish it were you that I hold here," Maggie calls down. "I'd love to have you in my hands again. Do you remember, Carla? "

I remember. It would be hard not to. I can recall the taste of the pomegranate seeds I was eating just before: the smoothness as I swirled each morsel around my mouth before crunching it to reveal the tart sweetness within. Maggie, on the other side of the cot, bit into the whole fruit, and the scarlet juice ran down her rose-tinged cheeks. Food was one the few allowable pleasures in the halls of the Academy. But when I reached out to wipe the red liquid away from her face, I could not stop myself from letting my fingers linger on stray strands of her blonde hair. It was soft to my touch, and I wanted to bury my face in it. I half-closed my eyes for fear of the look in hers.

Was it a miracle or a curse that Maggie's hand reached out and stroked my cheek? With an impish glance, she whispered hissing words and sparks of light shot from her fingertips. A parlour trick, our teachers called it, but they had no idea how strong the magic could be. My head knew that the red, green and blue sparks had no reality, that I should not feel them, but her slow touch left a trail of fire on my skin. I caught my breath and stifled a gasp.

The bits of light stopped, but Maggie's touch did not. She drew her hand under my chin, lifting it up and my lips parted of their own accord. Even without opening my eyes, I could see every detail of her face. I waited, wondering whether she would draw me nearer to her. I wanted to kiss her, to taste the bits of fruit on her tongue. I ought to pull away, I thought, but my body ignored my brain.

My breasts started to throb as they had never done before, and I inwardly begged her to pursue that warmth further, to let the narrow line of pleasurable heat cover every inch of my flesh. I opened my eyes wide and gazed deep into her, knowing full well the forbiddenness of what we both desired, and yet still wanting it.

"Aren't you the wicked, wanton one?" Maggie teased, but the laughter took the sting out of her words.

I tried to pull my hand away, but the effort was too much for me. Maggie caught my fingers in her grasp and squeezed. I felt the blood pulsing underneath, and even though there was no visible light I knew that she was sending her multi-colored sparks directly into my bones. I tingled, and laughed.

"I'm still hungry," she murmured, touching her red lips to the hollow in my throat. In all of my studies, in all of my reading, I never learned that such fiery power could come from the moistness of a woman's kiss. Certainly, the fumbling efforts of the boy students at the Academy had never generated these pulses through my nervous system.

Stars Inside Her 🌺

I reached out, arching my arms around her, wanted to pull her into myself. Her head jerked up, and I shuddered at the loss of contact. But her arms returned my embrace and we pulled toward each other. I could feel the solid connection as each part sought its own: breasts touching breasts, lips touching lips, thighs pressed against each other.

My teachers spoke often of the rhythm at the core of things, and I had no reason to doubt them. But until I felt that pulsing between my legs I had no reason to believe them either. As I felt the currents at the very center of my body, though, I knew they spoke truth. I shook the thought away. I didn't want to think about the teachings of the Sages. Not now, not here.

Maggie's hands pressed at my back, and I reciprocated. I drew her still closer to me, squeezing hard, but no matter how much strength I used it wasn't enough. I wanted her to become part of me, to become part of me, to meld into my essence so that we would not be two alone any more, but one single being of flesh. Our bulky student tunics blocked the connection, so we broke away from one another just long enough to struggle out of them. I luxuriated in the sensations of a faint breeze flowing across my naked buttocks and Maggie's living reality grounding me. I returned Maggie's kiss with a passion I'd never known I had.

Then, just as it seemed that, impossibly, we might be able to bridge the space between us, a too-harsh stream of light poured in from the door and washed over us. One of the Masters stood there, a frozen look of— anger?—on his face. Everything I felt drained into the cot, and all that was left was a sick dread. I wanted to

vanish, and even now, I wish I could erase my memory
of his contempt.

But Maggie took action. She caught me back into her
arms, turned me around to face her, and kissed me: defiantly, passionately. For a moment, the flood of power
returned. But from behind us I heard the Master's gasp,
and my back tingled. I broke free and twisted on the cot
to face the threat.

"Perversity!" The Master took a step towards us. "I
would never have expected it of you!"

I cringed. His eyes seemed to bore through my flesh,
seemed to see a deep cesspool in my head. I would have
done anything to stop that look. I could not lie; I could
not protest; I could not even speak. As if of its own accord
my body dropped to the floor, to the kneeling position
required of a penitent student.

I waited for Maggie to join me, but instead she
stood. The Master glared at her and insisted, "You know
the rules, not just of this Academy, but of magic. 'Like
with like' is an abomination!"

Maggie shook her head. "I don't believe it! 'That
which is, is by nature right.'"

Part of me admired her willingness to fight back, to
challenge the Master with the words of the Eternal Writ
itself. However, most of me wanted her to be quiet, to
join me on the floor. A time of penance and it would be
as if the incident never happened. I didn't dare speak, but
inside I pleaded with her to be submissive.

I could have saved my energy. Maggie walked to the
door. "I'm leaving," she said.

The Master frowned. "Maggie, you're one of our
most talented students, but that does not give you the

right to flaunt your mockery of scripture. Nor does it exempt you from repentance."

She whirled to face him. "I've done nothing to be ashamed of. I came here to learn magic, but so far all I've learned is how you want me to act. I'm tired of pretending and tired of all you too-holy masters. I'm leaving." As she turned away, her glance caught mine. "Come away with me, Carla."

I swallowed hard to ease my suddenly dry mouth and throat. "I can't."

The Master waved his hand, and she froze in midstep. "It's not that easy," the Master said.

Maggie cackles from the rafters. "Are you still doing penance, Carla?"

I pause before answering. In one sense, no—the physical side of the punishment was done long ago. But the lingering scars on my heart, they still cause pain. Every time one of my fellow students approaches me, every time I look up suddenly and see a Master standing there, every time I sleep and dream.

The mangled body of a small grey bird plummets to my feet. It squeaks once, then lies silent. I can feel the last life energies escaping. I look up at the bridge. "My penance isn't anything compared to yours."

She answers me with a shriek.

I see her for the first time: a solid blackness in the dark. Her eyes glow red but little else about her is clear. I imagine that she still maintains the form of a woman, but I can't be sure. Perhaps that is just my own desires speaking.

"Betrayer!" she screams at me. "You testified against me!"

"I didn't know." I protest. "They swore you would only be banished."

Maggie laughs bitterly. She sounds too much like she did when the Parade of Justice stopped underneath this gate all those years ago. The Most Senior Sage faced her then and demanded, once again, a statement of repentance. Maggie refused, of course, talking her stand with her arms crossed and legs solidly apart.

He didn't look at all surprised, and nodded his head. Two acolytes stripped her of her enveloping mage robes, letting the black cotton cloth fall to the ground. Despite the stern injunctions to me to keep my head bowed during the Parade, I snuck a peak at her. Even clad only in a simple white shift, Maggie still was beautiful.

I waited for the Sage to order her outside the boundaries of the Academy. Instead all of the senior members of the faculty formed a circle around Maggie.

"You are too dangerous for us to allow you to leave," the Sage said, "And too dangerous for us to allow you to stay. Therefore, you are sentenced to remain between the worlds."

Of course, she fought, but the efforts of a student mage were futile against the combined efforts of adepts. Strong chains of words and light wove around her and a blanket of darkness covered her mouth. The Most Senior Sage ran his hands over her body with what seemed like a gloating pleasure, lathering it with ointment. He took too long a time in rubbing the pink substance over her breasts and deep into her private crevices.

Then each faculty member in turn etched a mark on her, starting with Old Master Ecker who reached out with a barely concealed disgust and scratched at her with his ancient claws, and ending with Master Gyy who beamed from underneath tousled locks as he performed his first official act in academia.

I tried not to watch; but something in me told me that if I didn't, the not-knowing would haunt me forever. So I saw the moment when the final words were spoken and Maggie transformed into a thing.

She tried to fly away, but the wards held and she was imprisoned under the gate.

"Coward!" She taunts me from above.

"Why won't you give in?" I'm almost surprised to hear the words coming from my lips.

"And become like you? A tame mage?"

"I'm not a mage yet." Frustration edges into my voice, enough so that even I can hear it.

I may never be one. The Masters keep telling me that I have enough talent to make choices that few other students have, but something holds me back from the fullness of the Mysteries. They blame everything from laziness to willfulness, but I know that the block is Maggie. No amount of purgation gets rid of the dreams.

"Why did you come here?" Maggie shrieks.

"To ask you to repent."

"No. Now go away before I kill you."

"Please, Maggie, I care about you. All you need to do..."

She throws herself against the lowest rafter, and howls as the barriers hold. "How can you say you care?"

"It's true."

"Prove it!"

The bell from the Academy clock tower chimes one long slow peal after another, and the sound penetrates even here. Strange that I've never noticed before how loud the ringing is. Automatically, I count. Eleven o'clock. The faculty meeting that will rule again on my fitness meets at noon. I don't want another repetition of that ongoing purgatory; another time of standing there with bowed head admitting that mastery has once more eluded me.

I stare into the rafters. "How?"

"Say it up here. To me. Directly."

"And leave the ground? So that you can ... hurt me?" The real words stay locked in my throat.

Her voice is sensual again. "I wouldn't hurt you, Carla. I care about you too. I promise."

I know I can't believe her. I also know I can't continue on forever walking the path I've been on. One way or another, I do have to face her.

The gate beams are rough under my hands as I start to climb. Slowly, carefully, I inch up, feeling the strain in my arm muscles as I pull my weight up a bit at a time. I feel for footholds; and every time the slick leather of my boots slip, I gasp. Breathing becomes more difficult I don't dare look either down or up.

The ground starts to feel very far away. Above me, Maggie chortles with victory.

"That's it, Carla. Keep coming."

One hand at a time, I reach higher. Shivers cascade down my shoulders, chilling my back and converging in my stomach. I try to focus on the reality of the beams and the iron nails.

Halfway up, I pause for breath. I'm still safe but I won't be for long if I keep climbing. I could always stop, I know that.

"Carla?" There is something I can't interpret in Maggie's voice.

"Maggie?" I want to ask her so much, but all can say is her name. I start climbing again.

The darkness surrounds me as I finally reach the rafters, Maggie's domain. I cling to my foot-wide wooden perch, and wait for her. A thin tendril of black appears first, clutching a bloody feather. I tremble, but I stay.

The tendril moves closer to my face and strokes the side of my face with the feather. "You're still so beautiful," Maggie whispers.

I reach up and touch the blackness. It is surprisingly warm, like the fur of a cat that has been in the sun or like the mug holding a cup of tea. My fingers pass through it, but I try to make the touch a caress.

More of her comes into focus. She is close, her form matching my own crouch. I can almost see the features on her face, and I do not know how to read them. Maggie's hands reach out—real hands now, not just tendrils—and yank at the buttons on my tunic. Each time she pulls, I fear that I will lose my balance and fall.

"Stop it, Maggie."

"Stop it?" she mocks. "Why? I don't see a Master around. It's finally safe to finish what we started."

"We're... 'Like with like is an abomination.'" I recite. I've had a lot of time to have those words beaten into my head.

The red eyes materialize and they are blazing. "Like?" she hisses. "Like? Carla, you have no idea how unlike we are. You're weak and cowardly, and I hate you."

She pushes me back on the beam. The force of the landing knocks the wind out of me, and I cannot even scream to protest. My arms swing into empty space, but my head and my shoulders balance precariously on the wood. The blackness that is Maggie swirls over me, entering my mouth and squeezing at my breasts. She reeks of blood. And anger.

I try to fight back, but there is nothing there to fight against.

Her fury is real, though, and it hammers at the places I most want to guard. I've always been weaker than Maggie: in physical strength, in will, in the potential for magic. Given time, she will win.

If ever I needed the power of the Mysteries, I need it now. Use what you have inside, the Masters often chide me. Desperation courses through my body, and prickles as it runs through my chest. I close my eyes and try to channel it through my hands. I can feel the tingle as it reaches my fingers.

Maggie presses herself against me as I reach up through her. Somewhere in the darkness that surrounds her I make contact with pure energy. It flows in a circle that uses my arms as a path: shining energy followed by desperation, followed by more power.

I have done it! After all these years, I have finally tapped the heart of the Mysteries. I can go back to the Masters in triumph now. And if I want to, I think, I could destroy Maggie here and now. Maybe that would end the dreams.

She has pulled away from me and now lurks on the far side of the beam. I use my hands to steady myself on it. But as I do, some of the power flows out of the cycle. Looking down, I see that something gritty has formed beneath me. Dirt. Like a thick snowfall, it covers the surface of the beam.

It takes me a moment to realize that it means safety. She cannot hurt me as long as I touch the earth it represents. We are equals up here now, she and I.

I look at her. She could have retreated into the rafters, away from my touch. Instead Maggie stands there defiant and waiting. I take a step forward and pause. "Come here," I say.

"And have you obliterate me?" she asks. Her voice isn't trembling.

"Coward," I mock gently and take another step. It is not easy to walk on the earth-covered beam, but I'm not afraid.

Maggie meets me in the middle. I start unbuttoning my tunic where she left off.

"What are you doing?"

I smile. "You spoke true words," I tell her. "We are very unlike. So, that which is, is by nature right."

I let the student tunic fall, barely seeing it as it tumbles to the ground far below. A breeze teases at my bare skin, as I step out of the tights and boots as well. Maggie stands there motionless while I undress.

My thighs tingle. And then she swoops toward me. Her lips meet mine and her essence wraps around my tongue. Her breasts press against my chest. I embrace her, trying to encompass all of her in my arms. She strokes my back, my hair, my buttocks. I pull her closer.

Her black form penetrates into my body and then pulls out again. I can barely stand the initial pain, but I don't want her to stop.

"Again," I moan.

Maggie comes at me again, fully immersing herself in me. Again and again, we come together and separate. Time becomes immaterial, lost in this ebb and flow of our substances. How strange to have ecstasy not limited to one small part, but diffused over the whole body. I pant and then scream with the absolute joy.

She screams too and totally enters me. For a long minute, we are two-in-one, Maggie/Carla/Maggie/Carla. Then she pulls away and we sink down to the beam together.

Maggie seems more solid somehow. "I'm sorry," she whispers. "I'm sorry."

"Hush," I tell her. "It's all right."

"Don't leave me."

I don't know how to answer her. I am spared from answering by a sudden fluttering of wings. A pair of orange birds fly toward us, slowing as they pass within reach. Maggie watches them but she makes no move to stop either one.

"Don't leave me," she repeats.

I stretch out my arms to her, and hope that the invitation I cannot speak is readable on my face. She stares at me with dawning hope, and then ever so gently merges herself again into me. Her blackness soaks into my skin, and I welcome her with an open heart. It feels strange, as if I have become pregnant with a child who refuses to be confined to the womb. I inch my way along the beam to the side of the bridge.

And then we start the climb down.

CROW HILL
Kat Beyer

I once followed a blue-eyed, black-haired woman all the way from Seattle to Scotland. I arrived in Edinburgh without so much as a penny to masturbate with: this was my second mistake. Or perhaps it wasn't a mistake; if I had been rich, I might have taken longer to find out what kind of person I thought I was in love with. And more importantly, if I had been rich I might never have noticed Arthur's Seat on the way to work. I might never have seen what I saw up there.

As soon as it was apparent that she wasn't going to find the sort of job she wanted right away, blue-eyed, black-haired Jess lapsed into a sullen funk and started smoking a pack a day. Everybody knows that hard times can show you what people are made of, but somehow I could never believe that her unbelievable body did not house a matching soul. So I stayed, and wore out a pair of shoes walking into every pub in town asking for work. I was finally hired by a pub that sat on the Royal Mile in

119

the middle of the city. Tits speak an international language, and mine tend to make lewd suggestions even when I don't want them to.

Pub work is not for the faint of heart, or for those who object to being groped nightly. You have to have a mouth that can run on autopilot, dispensing wit, refusing propositions, and staying out of political arguments while your mind tracks fifteen drink orders, five sandwiches in the toaster oven, and the state of the rather violent regular in the corner. He's going to start hitting someone just when you've got four Guinesses settling on the spilltray. (Tell Sooz to start a new keg of eighty shilling, and we're running out of tonic water. And bring up another bottle of Bunnahabhain if we've got one.) Your lungs have to be fit for breathing a haze of smoke and sweat that leaves little room for oxygen. And when the fights start around ten o'clock, those two soldiers you've been cultivating on the left side of the bar will have to be sent into action to break them up, or at least move them out into the street.

Despite all that, some good, sound Scots came there to drink. I liked them, and I liked talk before the place got so crowded you couldn't hear yourself think; I liked chatting with Sooz and Euan while we swept up, and I didn't actually mind cleaning the bathrooms after closing. But that world of noise and smoke addled my mind and left me flat exhausted at the end of the day. I had no energy to think of a way up out of it. I had to work on keeping the job.

Gold summer turned into wet winter. I worked hard and came home bathed in beer and cigarette smoke. I remember that I stopped seeing color. This wasn't because of all that grey Scottish rain; I stopped seeing color because my endless dull struggle had bleached my life. There was never enough money and never ever enough Jess. But I know people have been more miserable than I was, and I think it's a rotten shame. It's no life, keeping your mind clenched around your few pound coins so you can make it through to the next day. It tires you out until you've nothing left; this is what the rich don't understand. The rich can afford rest. The rich can afford color.

Certainly there was no color in the flat. All our roommates were just as tired as we were, and as soon as I crossed the threshold into the room Jess and I shared, my thoughts, not very coherent in the first place, would tangle up in the mess of Jess. She'd snap at me for all kinds of imagined slights, and I would think, yes, she's right about this one and that one, but I didn't mean to, I didn't know; and I would lean against the doorframe trying to figure it all out. Other times she would get up from the couch where she was watching TV, and take my pay right out of my hand where I stood on the doorstep.

"I'm going to the all-night. We're out of bread and milk," she would inform me, and, sticking her cigarette between her lips, she would shrug on her coat and walk out the door. I got as much thanks as the Tory government that grudgingly handed her a dole check.

"Jess—" I would plead sometimes, and she would see she was losing me. Then she'd let her fingers travel down, softly stroking my jeans. She'd take a long drag from her cigarette with her other hand, and blow the strands of smoke all around us like a spell. She'd take my zipper between finger and thumb and work it open slowly, still smoking.

"Hold still," she'd say, parting her lips to release another thin stream of smoke. "And keep your mouth shut."

I wouldn't move. I'd need her fingers there. She'd just stroke me right above my clitoris; she knew damn well where it was, but she wasn't going to actually bother to touch it.

I would always end up kneeling in front of her by the bay window in our room. She liked to be seen from the street, even though we were three storeys up. She would shake down her long dark hair and open her shirt to me, so that I could see those round tight nipples. She hadn't let me touch them for a long, long time. It still stuns me to think how much energy it must have taken, to be so careless and cruel. But I think that life was hard enough that it would have taken more energy to be kind than cruel.

I would open her pants and pull them down and lick her just so, the same way every time, the way I knew she'd liked in the past; I was too tired to create, to think, to play with this body I adored in my worn-out way.

When she was finished we would go to bed and I would lie awake until sleep was the only choice left. I don't know if she slept or not; she turned her back to me and didn't move, and her breathing slowed down. I always turned my face to the window. Up over the rooftops I could see the clouds riding in with unreal, impossible speed from the Firth. Though the window panes rattled a little, the winds were far wilder up there, wild and mad. The clouds shredded and re-formed, lit from underneath by the pinkish glow of the city lights, streaming endlessly past the rows of chimneys.

I waited for Jess to wake up, to roll over and smile like in the old days, to burst the dim room with midnight sun. But she didn't. And I had no sun of my own left, or so I thought.

I remember the night I first started seeing color again. It couldn't have been much past the spring equinox; I remember noticing that the sun was still up while I walked to my evening shift. I came out onto the Meadows on my way toward the Mile, and looked up. I realized that I had completely missed out on the fact that right in the middle of the city of Edinburgh there is a mountain. It's a volcanic cone, and it rises out of the city, shrugging off the blackened granite houses and holding its unstoppable green slopes up to the air. Like many hills all over Britain, it is called Arthur's Seat. As I stared at it, the sun struck its green shoulder and my world was full of sound and color again; I noticed that footballers and cricketers were springing up like daffodils all over the Meadows, shouting and sweating in the late evening light. I wondered where I had been all those months. It was someone else who had been walking from the smoke-filled flat to the smoke-filled pub and back.

I stood looking at Arthur's Seat for a long time. Finally I turned, and continued my walk into town to the Mile. For weeks I forgot, until one evening when I came home from a day shift and found that Jess had gone out with some friends. I sat alone in the silent flat for some time, staring absently at our collection of jam jars full of cigarette ash, until finally I got up, went out, and started walking towards Arthur's Seat. I played tag with the mountain, losing it among the high Victorian stone houses, finding it rising up again where my path led through a park; finally no more buildings stood between us. I came up against the wrought-iron fence of Holyrood Park and gripped the iron in both hands, wanting to cry. After a moment I decided not to give in yet. I walked the edge of the fence until I found a way in, and started up Queen's Drive where it spiraled towards the peak.

As I walked I was passed by pensive businessmen in Jaguars and pensive joggers in expensive jogging shorts. The wind from the Firth picked up, turning the long grass on its back, and my hair snaked about me and stung my face. I didn't tie it back. Up here, in the silence on the hill, I had this crazed idea that I would strangle some important force if I tried to tie my hair back with a rubber band.

The sun was hanging low over the city, lingering because it had plenty of time. The wind had blown the morning's rain clouds away. You could see everything, the whole world: Edinburgh as far as Queensferry, the Pentland Hills blueing in the south; on the north side, the Firth of Forth, and beyond, the North Sea already almost lost in the dusk. The road leveled out and I discovered that there is another whole world at the top of Arthur's Seat, a mild wilderness inside the city, with fields of long grass waving, and a loch with swans settling on it, cupped by the hills. Higher still, towering in the near distance, the two peaks of the cone rose above me: Crow Hill and Arthur's Seat. I climbed a low rise away from the road and sat down, looking out as far as I could and surveying the land I had suddenly inherited. I watched an oil tanker skirt the coast as it sailed up the Firth; I watched the clouds turn and wheel, and the birds circle below them; I watched cars skid through the streets, or creep where the rush hour traffic caught them.

Somewhere far down there, someone was swearing that there was more than a quarter-inch head on his Guinness, and I wasn't serving him. I hugged my knees to my chest and ignored the damp grass soaking my jeans. I hadn't had much exercise outside of pub work lately, and it's a stiff climb up that hill. I was a little tired, but my mind had cleared a bit, what with the air and the blood rushing about inside me. I could smell again, and think again.

To the west, in the center of town, a light bloomed suddenly on Calton Hill. I stared at it for a while, wondering if one of the government buildings was on fire; but then I had to conclude that someone was lighting a bonfire down there. I was surprised you were allowed to do that.

"Strange," I said aloud. "Strange, but cool."

"What's strange?" a woman asked nearby.

I almost rolled down the hill in shock. I had thought I was alone.

"The fire there," I explained, pointing.

She came and stood beside me.

"That?" she said, following my hand. "That's the May fire."

"They're allowed to light bonfires on Calton Hill?"

She laughed. She had a laugh that made me feel as if I could dart like a blackbird down the long expanse of grass. She smelled good, too; she wasn't hiding the smell of her body under a hundred expensive synthetic odors, but wearing some grassy scent that made you want to put your nose against her skin. I hadn't had the energy to notice so much about one person in many months. She smiled at me, a young woman, about my age maybe, with long soft hair; and she said, "Why not? It's a custom older than those who would stop it, I can tell you. Don't you celebrate May Eve where you come from?"

"I don't think I've even heard of it."

"You ought to go down to the fire down there, and celebrate tonight. The beginning of summer is something to celebrate," she added, smiling at me again. "And you might get yourself a lover. You never know."

"Already have one of those, and it isn't doing me any good," I answered, smiling ruefully.

"No," she told me gently. "You do not. You do not really have a lover, I think."

I could have been angry with this stranger, or taken offense that she presumed to know about my life. But the kind way she spoke gentled all anger out of me, and left only grief. I just pressed my lips together and nodded silently. I turned back to look at the fire on the hill below, down in the city; it winked in and out of the dark at me, and I realized that the sun had set. I thought the woman had gone, so still was the air beside me, but at last she said, "Now they will be closing the park. And you should go down. But if I were you, I wouldn't. No, I wouldn't."

"I should," I answered, as if this whole conversation were completely logical. "I should. It's dark, and it will be getting dangerous."

"Well, if you wait much longer, you must stay up here, and celebrate May Eve beneath Arthur's Seat."

I turned towards her slowly, finding her eyes by their glint in the dark.

"What do you mean? Are you warning me?" I asked.

"No, not warning you, no. Telling you what will happen."

I stood there, looking at the orange light on Calton Hill, remembering some remark a friend had made, about spending the night on Calton.

"Will you lead me down the hill?" I asked, looking into the faint reflections of her eyes. I wasn't really asking her to take me back down to the bottom of Holyrood Park, but I couldn't bring myself to say the words.

She understood anyway, and said, "Yes, I will lead you."

She took my hand and tugged me down the grass towards Arthur's Seat, and I knew we weren't going down into the city. Her hand was warm and smooth. As I watched, a tiny thread of golden light crept from between her fingers and wandered, like a torchlit procession, over my hand and into the night. I stared at it for a moment, and a finger of fear crept up my back. But then I knew as sure as my own blood in my veins that I would follow her hand where it led. We went on down the hill into the heart of Arthur's Seat.

I realized how cold it was with the night wind blowing in off the Firth now, and I was glad when we stepped down into a bowl of grass and out of the whirling air. I heard voices on the slope below us. My senses, silent for so long, told me now that there were quite a few people moving around down there. Someone called out to the woman and she answered, her voice starting suddenly out of the dark beside me; the notes of her words dropped through the grass, and she got a laughing reply. I didn't hear what was said because at that moment, I saw sparks fly up below, lighting up the underside of someone's hands; and then a flame tickled and grew until I could see the pile of wood it fed upon. In another moment the wood, impossibly dry on this damp day, flared up into a roaring fire that lit up the vale of grass and shone on the shoulder of Arthur's Seat. In the rippling light I saw many people milling around, and asked again, "Don't you have to get a permit for something like this? Won't they come and stop you?"

The woman grinned and replied, "Them that can see it, won't stop it."

A man came towards us, one side lit up with orange firelight. I stared at him, too, for on the dark side of his skin gold veins crept and wormed before evaporating in the darkness. He brought a plate and a cup and offered them to us. I looked down, seeing a half loaf of bread and a honeycomb, and smelling something sweet and strong in the cup. I ran my fingers along the rim of the cup, a red earthenware goblet with a pattern of notches cut into its rough unglazed surface. The last time I'd seen that kind of pottery I had been standing in a museum, at the beginning of a long timeline of British history. I looked hard at my companions, seeing at last the fey touch to their features, and comprehending the gold fire that trailed off them into the night. I said, "I think I know who you are. Will I have to stay forever if I eat this food?"

"Absolutely not!" the man laughed. "You think we'd want to be up to our ears with your kind? Present company excepted, of course," he added politely. "Here, come and eat. We're going to start soon."

But the woman laid a hand on my arm and said, "No; she's coming with me."

The man stopped and looked at her.

"Oh, aye," he answered. "Crow Hill."

I tried to ask him what he meant, but ended up cawing instead. I found myself slowly rising up above the man. He looked up at me, his face turning slowly with the land beneath me, smiled, and winked. The noise in the valley sank down and the stars wheeled around me. I had acquired a pair of black wings which carried me up the streams of air that ran round the mountain. The woman flew beside me, her eyes the same despite her new crow-form.

"I don't generally do crows at night, but I thought it would be appropriate," she said; and to this day I do not know how she was speaking to me, whether inside my mind, or with her own voice, or in crow-speak.

Maybe you've read about people changing into animals. Perhaps you have been changed yourself once or twice. I never had; I never even believed it could happen. But if you've experienced it, you'll know what I mean when I say that the whole air was alive to me. My body was bathed in the currents; I knew how to ride them the way the clouds know. We flew up to the peak and when we landed, our own shapes again, every hair on my skin prickled with the knowledge. And while I stood that way, every skein of wind on the mountain working its way through my clothes and around each hair of my body, while I stood knowing each inch of me in the wind— while I stood wide open to the world, the woman turned to me and filled up the world with a kiss.

⚜ *Stars Inside Her*

I thought I knew everything about her mouth when she finished; I just stood before her, breathless. She smiled at me, and took my hand again, and said only, "Look."

We were very high up. The city mirrored the sky with its thousand lights; the fire on Calton Hill flickered back and forth as if signaling to the bonfire we had so recently stood beside, below Arthur's Seat. But then, while I watched, the city lights blinked out, one by one, and the buildings sank and the trees rose up to cover it all, except for a fire here and there: the one on the shoulder of the Seat, the one on Calton Hill, another where the Castle should have been, and others, further west. I saw people gathering around all of these, and I knew that I saw both people long gone around the fires, and many more people who were alive now. I knew that if I were down there, I would recognize faces from the street, from work, from shops and high windows. They were there whether their daylight selves knew it or not.

The woman said, "You see the world like this just for a moment because in your people's hearts you have not forgotten, no matter where you are or who you are, or whether you were ever told; because the love still burns in you, for the land your mother, for the kin you are to each other; even while you struggle and stumble, fouling things up and trying to mend them."

The wind blew around us, bringing the sounds of the fires we watched, the voices and the music. Another night I would have wanted to join them, but I could feel her standing behind me, as I had once felt the touch of my lover's voice on the nape of my neck.

What about Jess, what about our bond, lying like a corpse between us? You be the judge. I only know what I did. I just stood, and waited for the woman's mouth again.

She came up just behind me, and spoke softly to the hairs on my neck, saying, "What do you want?"

I took a deep breath.

"You," I said.

"Then wait for the offering. Get rid of your clothes."

I did, though my fingers didn't seem to know what to do with the buttons and zippers. She only watched, sitting in the street clothes that were just another shapechange to her. Then she filled a cup with mead and held it to my lips where I sat. I opened my mouth and let it run down my throat, sweet and burning. I swallowed and lay back with my head full of gold. The stars seemed awfully busy rearranging themselves.

"Why are they doing that?"

"Why are what doing what?"

"The stars. They won't hold still."

"They never do, you know. But it's probably the mead."

"Ah."

She laughed again and I wanted to step inside that one sound and stay there all night, bouncing around like a lark in a field. All at once she wriggled out of her clothes like an irritable snake sick of a tight skin. I will never see a body like that again, but I'm not sure I mind; some things humans just aren't meant to comprehend, and I think that her body is one of them. She has tits with those ferociously enticing curves to them, you know the ones, that swell like fat sea waves and then throw two hard nipples up in the air as if gravity is something that happens to other breasts. Her belly is better than the taste of mead, a sweet smooth honey-pot that leads you straight down to the gold hair between her legs. She has long, muscular arms and legs, and long fingers that are made to get up to no good. And the golden tracers twine around her skin and into the air, like worshipful glow-worms.

She dipped her fingers in the mead and presented them to my lips. I wanted to take those long slender fingers all the way into my mouth, but she only let me have the mead-soaked tips. Then she dipped them in the mead again and began to draw on me. I waited patiently now, inhaling over and over the heavy honey scent, sharp-sweet, the strangest wine in the world. Her fingers slipped lightly over me and again there was nothing in the universe but the place where they touched my skin, sometimes one finger-pad, sometimes two or three, dipping away into the cup, and returning, sliding slowly and deliberately.

She covered me in mead-drawings. I couldn't see the patterns for the liquid barely stained my skin. But when she had at last painted even the soles of my feet and skin behind my ears, the glow-worms traveled down her hands and went to work. The instant they touched the mead they turned it to gold light that spread faster than fire. In an instant my skin shone with golden knotwork patterns and spirals, of a kind at once cruder and more complex than those I had seen everywhere in Celtic art. I laughed, turning my glowing hands over. I could feel the warm mead and the cool spaces of untouched skin in between.

Then she dipped her fingers in mead once more, and slid them down into the one unlit triangle on my body. She painted tiny knotwork on my cunt and my mons venus. The fire trails ran in and out of my hair like tracks in a forest. All I could do was shut my eyes and open my mouth.

When she was finished I saw she had connected each spiraling line to the patterns covering the rest of me. When every spiral was spun and every knot tied, the light began to pulse. It began where my heartbeat now resided, right inside my clit. And from there it beat outwards, fanning through the lines, now soft, now bright, now soft, now bright.

I stood up, spreading my arms wide and spreading my legs to the wind, and I laughed. The pulse of light shot up my chest and down my thighs, regular and fierce as my newfound heart could make it. The woman sat and looked up at me, smiling, the tips of her fingers burning gold.

"You're summoning them," she told me.

"I am? Who?" I turned around, suddenly full of fear. What would happen to me now, marked and—prepared—like this? She stood up and touched my shoulders.

"It is not that kind of offering you will make," she said. "It's another kind, nearly as frightening in its way. You'll be fine. You are fine, so fine..." she added, smiling again, and kissed my throat. I felt her mouth's pulse on my jugular vein; our pulses spoke to each other with that dark thump that says, over and over, "One; one; one..." So of course I didn't hear the fox that came up behind us, touching her red flank and uncurling as a woman. I didn't hear the owl that dropped down into a woman's form, fingers still outstretched like wing tips, or the doe that turned into a longlegged, slender girl, or any of the others who came to us.

Once more the windy black air opened out in front of me, and I felt all the height of the peak; then once more, like the contraction of a heart, the world narrowed down to just this, tawny forms and firm muscles, soft mouths. We went to our knees in the grass. Our legs just couldn't hold us up anymore. I guess lust made our joints loose. And there in the grass we were, feeling the scraping kiss of it on our backs and the warmth of each other on our fronts. I lost track of everything: myself, the star's beat, the place between my mouth and the skin of my nearest lover.

Somewhere in the middle of this the woman came to me. She stood over me and I knelt right beneath her, as I once had with Jess; but she was so sweet to taste, it was as if my tongue was drawn up into her. I had to lick every soft fold. I had to pull her tits down to my mouth and take each one as far in as I could, and then lick and tease around each nipple, standing my tongue on its tip. I slid down again and pushed my mouth in between her legs until one of us was crying out, and it took me a while to realize it was her. On her last shout she grabbed me by the hair and threw me to the ground—not as hard as you might think—and fucked me there. She fucked me with her mouth, while the stars shook out the sky above and the wind wailed around Crow Hill. She had a sly tongue; it tracked me down like a hound; it found the secret place, the swollen bottom side of my clit, and drew my pulse out from my mouth, where it had traveled, and back into my cunt. I pushed my head back in the grass and opened my legs until I felt her hot hands on my ass, restraining me, keeping me from grinding as hard as I had to. I had to, but she held me open there, and still, so I had to endure her tongue while it slipped down and rimmed me, and ran backup to taste me again.

She slid her belly up between my wet legs and then rested on me, chest to chest. I reached out and pulled her head down and kissed her, wrapping my thighs against her waist, feeling the muscles of her stomach move against my thighs like the muscles of some strong fish.

I could hear the inside of her; I could hear her whole body speak, and it told me all about the spring and the reason for May Eve. I rested my head on the grass and she looked down at me, quietly. All around us the others were stroking and calling; sometimes their hands slid out of the tangle to touch us where we lay at the center. But we had forgotten them just for the moment.

She fed me bits of honeycomb and sips of mead, still pressing against me where we lay, and letting my clit throb slowly against her. Then there were many hands sliding up underneath me, lifting me up in the air; I could feel someone's tongue in my cunt again but soon I couldn't concentrate even on that. There were tiny orgasms beginning right in the center of my groin, but they didn't stop there. They raced around over my skin, following the paths lit up for them. Every time one struck a spiral I would begin to cry out with pain and pleasure because I could feel it coming on, spinning round and round down to the center of the spiral, building up unbearably and unstoppably until I cried out again. I came in my hands and the soles of my feet, the backs of my knees, the skin inside my belly button. I came in my eyelids, over and over, held up to the stars and shouting until my throat was hoarse. I came at the tips of the hair on my skin. And then the hands let go in a slow collapse and I landed right in the center of these golden women. We shouted out the earth's best and lewdest joke, fucking the spring in.

After a while I fell asleep, surrounded by tired lovers. Despite the strength coursing through us and the liquid taste of our pulses against each other, we were exhausted. The stars had wheeled pretty far around when someone woke me and we stretched and rose, rubbing each others' sore muscles.

We went down the hill together, carrying empty jars and plates, brushing close to one another. I pulled on my clothes at the burnt-out bonfire, and as my shirt slipped over my head, I smelled sweat and grass and spilled mead and woodsmoke. I looked down and saw that the patterns still glowed through the fabric.

"They'll fade when the sun comes," the woman told me.

She took my head in her hands and kissed me once more, letting the world out by the way it had come in. The others put their arms around us and one by one I kissed my lovers goodbye, with tears starting in my eyes. They only smiled at me and brushed the corners of my eyes, stroking the saltwater at the hollows in their necks in some mysterious salute.

Then she put her smooth, soft hand in mine, and led me down the slope. It was still dark, and I couldn't tell you what path we followed; we seemed to go straight down towards the lights by the University and the Mile.

But when I came back later, I saw the steep heights of the Salisbury Crags, and could not tell how we came down those treacherous cliffs so smoothly. At the foot of the park, I turned and held her one more time. We didn't speak, and she laid her head in the curve of my neck.

"What will I remember you by?" I asked finally.

She lifted her head and grinned at me in the dark.

"I give you all the daffodils," she said. "You'll remember us."

I stepped away, not really ready to go.

"In your stories," she said suddenly, "in your stories about us, you always say we exact some price of you—perhaps several years have passed in your own world when you return to it, or perhaps we take a child—but the truth is, we exact only one price of you. And it is a terrible one, to be true. Because the price is that when you leave us you will no longer be content with things as they are."

She stopped and looked me full in the face, eyes amber and then green.

"Remember one more thing: remember what you saw on Arthur's Seat. Remember it when you lie down with someone, and when you stand by a fire, and when you walk down the street or under a grove of trees; carry it with you. Because you were not shown that for nothing. You were not made for the sorrows you've had. You were made for something else. Carry what we gave and you gave, and go find it.

"And remember," she added at last, as the light began to creep up on us, "you have been blessed. Walk like you have been blessed, and the things you have lost will come back to you again."

I knew I would not be able to hold her one more time.

"You take care of yourself," I said, though I knew it was a silly thing to say to such a one. "Will I ever...?"

She laughed.

"Who knows? Not all this spring and summer, certainly. We've got all sorts of places to go, so much to do. Who can ever tell?"

And again I knew she was more kin to the grass and the birds than my kind. My kind say to each other, "Call me tonight," as if death will never take either of us away. I looked at the mountain rising behind her.

"Goodbye," I said.

"Goddess by you," she answered, smiling, and turned to walk back into her hills.

I could hear the early morning sounds beyond the park now. I climbed over the piddling wrought iron fence that somebody thinks keeps people out, and went up the streets back towards Marchmont, not really sure why I was headed that way. When I turned a corner the breeze brought the smells of my shirt up to me, and the woodsmoke tingled in my nostrils. It came as a relief to me that, with a shirt stinking so marvelously, I'd have a hard time lying my way out of this one.

On the sleepy streets I found myself thinking and seeing what I had not before. Flowers in a shop window made me drunk. Red mailboxes cheered me. Stupid, colorful ads in bus shelters, smells from pancake houses, everything ran up into my senses shouting and throwing the furniture in my mind around. I thought about trying for a job at an old friend's company, and wondered why I hadn't considered doing that earlier. It was good work, shipping and selling things people could really use, like cookware properly made, long-lasting tools. I smelled bread being pulled from the ovens at the all-night bakery. As I passed a baker loading a truck, he smiled at me, reached down into one of the crates and handed me a morning roll.

"That's for being the most beautiful woman I've seen all day," he told me.

"Well, it's early yet," I laughed.

"So let it be a lucky day," he grinned, and went back to work.

I thought of the woman who might be waiting at home, and felt sorry for her; if she was worried about me, she would chew it all up in hard words for me. But as I turned down Melville Drive I knew my mind was made up. I could sleep over at a friend's until I found a new place. And then, because nothing could stop it, the sun rose over Arthur's Seat.

THE BLIZZARD'S DAUGHTER
Susanna J. Sturgis

Ilize was still a toddler when she noted how little she resembled her siblings, all of whom had their father's coffee brown hair, dark eyes, and skin that turned golden in the spring sun. "Why," she asked Jehan, her mother, "is my hair so much paler than theirs, my skin fairer, my eyes light grey when theirs are almost black?"

Jehan laughed aloud and told her, "Because you are the blizzard's daughter!"

Some years later Ilize understood this to mean that Merrell was not her sire, that Jehan had once (or twice) upon a time taken another man to warm her bed and body—on a frigid winter's night was a good guess, because Ilize had been born on the fall equinox. "Did he leave you then," Ilize asked, "or did you not love him truly?"

"Who would let a blizzard linger in her house?" Jehan countered. Ilize scowled and asked no more questions.

More years passed, and Ilize grew ever more different from her siblings and all the other folk she knew. Where they suffered winter's wild snow and dark cold, celebrating every smallest sign of coming spring, Ilize embraced the year's harshest season. For her feet she fashioned oblong frames of willow and thong and walked atop the deepest snow. When the village's store of venison and hare needed replenishing, even the hardiest young people found reason to delay; Ilize volunteered eagerly for the chance to roam abroad with bow, knife, and sling.

Being different, Ilize kept her own counsel and made her own rules. For companionship she preferred Neva and Sax, her dogs. Neva was the blinding almost-blue white of sun on fresh-fallen snow; Sax was the pearl grey of snow-laden sky. In shadow they seemed identical, with the same long fur, ruffed around the neck, silky on the belly, and watchful eyes the deep, ever-changing dark of thunderclouds. They went with her everywhere, Neva on her left, Sax on her right. Ilize built a sled with bear bones for runners and taught her dogs to pull it.

Jehan noticed her daughter's aloofness and neither discouraged nor fostered it. Though two of Jehan's younger children had already chosen partners, with a third likely to do so soon, Ilize showed little interest in her peers, either men or women, and was usually content to sleep alone in the small back room of her mother's house, her dogs alongside.

Then, on the longest night of her nineteenth year, while all through the country people built bonfires to rekindle the sun and drummed to wake it from its torpor, Ilize sat cross-legged on the black bear rug before her mother's raised stone hearth. Jehan sat beside the roaring fire restitching the toggles of her old parka and waited.

"I want to know my father," said Ilize.

"You are the blizzard's daughter," Jehan replied.

"I am a woman grown and have no more need of pretty stories," Ilize responded, impatience tingling in her arms.

"Truly," said Jehan, "you are the blizzard's daughter." And she rose and went into her own room. There she knelt beside an ornately carved, high-polished chest of hardwoods not found in that country and drew from it a statue, which she carried to the common room in gloved hands and set at the edge of the hearth. "This was the blizzard's gift for you, when you should ask about your origin."

It was an eagle, its every feather clearly etched yet soft to the eye. Ilize felt its eyes bore through her. What was it wrought of? Whiter than glass, yet crystalline, shimmering about the edges like diamond teardrops: Ilize had never seen its like. Entranced Ilize reached out to touch it, then yanked her fingers back. "It's cold!" she said.

"Of course it's cold!" Jehan smiled, her eyes gone distant; surely, thought her daughter, she is remembering nights passed with the sculptor. "It is made of snow and glazed with ice."

"Hah!" Ilize snorted. No snow sculpture could out-last the winter of its making. Did her mother really expect her to believe otherwise?

"It is," Jehan repeated, firmly this time, "made of snow. Ordinary snow—though, to be sure, its maker is not ordinary."

"I want to find my father."

"The eagle will guide you," said Jehan, and so Ilize understood that this was no common statue but one of great power.

The very next morning Ilize harnessed Neva and Sax to her sled, already packed with an axe, tinder box, sling, bow, and a dozen arrows, and a supply of dried fruit, waybread, and other provisions. At the front perched the snow eagle, its pedestal wedged among bundled furs. Ilize hugged her mother, strapped on her snowshoes, and headed north over the crusty snow, toward the vast for-est and, several days beyond, the Great North River. Beyond this she had never been, nor had anyone she knew. The eagle would have to show her the way.

To cross the Great North River—already frozen three arm-lengths deep—Ilize stowed her snowshoes and stood on the little platform set upon the runners at the back of her sled. Even with the added weight, the dogs ran easily. Ilize had thought to explore the unknown north bank of the river, but before she reached the fir-lined shore the snow eagle unfurled its wings partway and rose, facing up the river. When Ilize tried to maintain her course, the eagle extended its wings fully. Each was as wide as the sled was long. Though the dogs' pace did not slacken, the sled began to slow. Only when Ilize tight-ened Neva's near rein, pointing dogs and sled upriver, did the eagle furl its wings and settle back, a statue once more.

After seven days' steady progress, the eagle rose to guide them off the river and due north, into a trackless land whose scrubby trees and boulders, shallow valleys and slight hills were shrouded in snow. Ilize retrieved her snowshoes and floundered in and out of several deep drifts before noticing that the eagle was directing her, if she would but pay attention to its wings and beak. This she did, and found thereby the firmest footing. On some days snow and sky formed a seamless whole, with Ilize, her dogs and sled its only interruption. On others the sun's glare nearly blinded her, though it gave no warmth. The days were short, the nights and twilights long. Ilize saw no game, not even tracks, and as her provisions dwindled she wondered how she and the dogs would eat. All the while the eagle set her course.

Gradually earth appeared again, hard, stony, snowswept earth shadowed by lichen and broken by brave stands of stunted spruce and pine. The north wind ebbed and flowed but never stopped, ruffling the dogs' fur, the fur of Ilize's gloves and parka. When she stopped to rest, she turned Sax and Neva loose; they brought their catches back to her, but she let them keep the meat. For herself she brought down rabbits with her sling and scrounged wood enough to roast them in the lee of the sled.

She would have missed the house entirely had the eagle not risen to full height and wingspread to demand she look again at the raw hills passing on her left. Set into one was a doorway of carefully fitted uncaulked stones. What manner of person could live out here, days upon days from any fellow, on ground that even in high summer must be too hard to turn? An odd one surely, Ilize thought, but not one likely to do her harm; this place was far too desolate for human predators. Whatever, the snow eagle wanted her to stay: it had settled back and returned to ice once more. Ilize knocked tentatively on the wooden door, which was painted a deep velvety green. Silence. She rapped more sharply the second time. Again there was no answer.

She pushed the door open and called out: "Hello?"

Hearing nothing, she stepped warily into a round room so warm she immediately removed her gloves and unlaced her parka. The odors of baking bread and simmering stew enveloped her, and underneath it scents she had not smelled in months: those of a growing garden. The room's perimeter was dim, its center bright where a fire burned in a squat metal stove. On the round cobbled stone hearth sat a covered copper pot and beside it several oval loaves of dark bread. In a semicircle just within the firelight stood a dozen looms: some narrow, others as wide as Ilize was tall. On each a tapestry was nearing completion. Greens, grays, and browns were the weaver's favorite colors, or so Ilize thought until she came to the penultimate, in which a white mark appeared halfway up one side and spread till it dominated the rows at the unfinished end. The last was patterned white on white, like billowing clouds layered one upon another.

"So."

Ilize jumped back, her hand on the hunting knife sheathed on her belt.

The woman held her hands open at shoulder height and stepped carefully into the circle of brightest firelight.

She had come through a doorway that Ilize hadn't even seen, directly opposite the entrance in the shadowy back of the room. She was even taller than Ilize, broader in hip and shoulder, clad in brown leather leggings and matching sleeveless tunic over a green wool shirt. "Ilize Jehansdaughter," she said.

"Yes," said Ilize. Her hand moved away from her knife hilt.

"Good."

"The door was open."

"You were expected."

Questions crowded Ilize's throat: What is this place, and who are you, how could you expect me and how do you know my name? "The snow eagle brought me here," she said.

"Yes," said the woman. Her dark eyes were playful, though she did not smile, and the near-black braids that crowned her head glittered with silver.

How much should I say? Ilize wondered. How much does she know? If I ask, will she be angry?

"Sit," said the woman, nodding to a pile of cushions tumbled near the hearth. Ilize sat. Her fingers stroked the carpet absently then recoiled: what she sat upon was not fur or hide or woven wool but grass, thick and close-clipped. The woman served up two bowls of stew, and two loaves wrapped in brown cloth. "I am called Tierra," the woman said, seating herself so close to Ilize that their knees almost touched.

"My dogs . . . ?" Ilize asked.

"Neva and Sax have been cared for," Tierra answered.

Like her own, Ilize thought, Tierra's people, whoever they were, offered hospitality to wayfarers, whoever they might be, and postponed questions till the meal was done. The stew was hearty with venison, potato, and carrot, which didn't surprise her, but also green pepper and yellow corn, which did, these being summer vegetables and not known for keeping well. Like Tierra, she picked large morsels out with her fingers, lifted the bowl to her lips to sip the broth, and used torn hunks of bread to mop up the rest.

"So, Ilize Jehansdaughter," Tierra said, "you are a long way from home."

"Home?" asked Ilize. The word irritated her like a mosquito. "Can it truly be my home if my hair is fair where most are dark, if I am tall where most are short, if the rest think me strange to go abroad while they are huddled by their stoves?"

"Can it not be," Tierra countered, "when you have Jehan's dark and deep-set eyes, the set of her jaw, and her broad long-fingered hands?"

"Perhaps," said Ilize. "But my mother says I am the blizzard's daughter, not her partner Merrell's, and I have come seeking my father."

Tierra said nothing for a long time.

"It is true," Ilize said, her voice rising. "The snow eagle brought me here. I think the snow eagle must be magical, for no ordinary snow statue could have survived eighteen summers wrapped in my mother's wooden chest."

"Have no doubt about that," said Tierra. "But few seek the blizzards out; for most it is enough to wait, huddled by the stove as you say, and let the blizzards come to them."

Until that moment Ilize had assumed only one blizzard. So there were many, or at least more than one? It did make sense. But would she recognize her father, and he her? "Surely if I were not meant to come," Ilize said, thinking out loud, "the snow eagle would not have guided me."

"It is as you say," Tierra said. "Yet, in deepest winter? This is strange. In the morning we will venture forth, to the edge of the blizzards' country, and you will see for yourself."

"In the morning?" Ilize balked at delay.

"Would you travel in the dark?" Tierra raised her dark brows and smiled. "The sun has long gone west, and the moon won't rise till after midnight. The eagle rests, and so should you."

Settled in her makeshift bed of cushions and furs, Ilize realized that she knew not where the snow eagle slept, or her dogs, or her sled. She didn't know how Tierra made grass grow indoors, or how she came by peppers and corn in midwinter, or how this hard country yielded potatoes and carrots even when the days were long. Who was Tierra anyway? A weaver, certainly, but more than that. Some kind of shaman, Ilize guessed; how else would the woman know so much about her?

At first light, Ilize was already impatient to be gone, but Tierra set out oatmeal sweetened with dried fruit and cooled with cream, and bread still steaming with the heat of baking. Sax and Neva breakfasted on what looked like last night's stew. Ilize patted a place beside her, but the two dogs curled up at Tierra's side. Ilize bit her lip to block an ungracious remark.

Soon enough they were on their way. The snow eagle pointed them due north. While the hills that sheltered Tierra were still in sight behind them, they pushed through snow to Ilize's knees, then higher still. Ilize held the reins, Tierra close beside her on the driver's platform, but it was the eagle who guided the dogs. Had it not, they would have struggled through drifts to Ilize's chin and higher, and when land and sky mingled all around them—for soon it did, though it wasn't yet midmorning on what had been a cloudless day—Ilize knew that on her own she would have wandered endlessly in a great white circle.

When they stopped the sky was again pale blue, and stolid cliffs rose above the snowfields on either side, reaching northward left and right like two open hands. Between them turbulence shimmered, swirling back and forth like rushing clouds that meet a barrier in the sky and bounce back whither they have come. After a moment Ilize raised a forearm to guard her eyes.

"The blizzards' land," said Tierra.

Ilize peered across her arm. "There?" she whispered. "There."

Against her heart's caution, Ilize gathered her reins and chirruped to Sax and Neva. Tierra laid her hand on Ilize's but there was no need, for neither dog showed any sign of rising from its crouch. "Not until the vernal equinox will the way open to you," Tierra said. "While the night is longer than the day, the blizzards rule this land, and no human may cross it."

"I am the blizzard's daughter!" Ilize cried, with more bravado than good sense.

"So you are," agreed Tierra, "but see what the blizzard's gift tells you." The snow eagle sat as still as the statue it pretended to be.

"I don't care! I will go to seek my father!"

"You will not," Tierra said. "More, far more, is at stake here than what you want."

Without apparent movement, the sled now pointed south. Neva and Sax stood ready in their harness, and the snow eagle's wings were rising. Still, Ilize did not take kindly to being thwarted. She stepped back off the driver's platform and, to her astonishment, sank thigh deep in snow. With her second step she sprawled forward, and the cold stung her nose and mouth while the heat of her humiliation melted feathery crystals into an ice mask of her face.

Struggling not to laugh, Tierra pulled her up and out and with two bare hands covered Ilize's face. Those broad hands quickly warmed Ilize's skin and the blood beneath, already sluggish with cold. Belatedly, Ilize realized that her rash impulse might have killed her. Winter was not forgiving anywhere, least of all on the marches of the blizzards' land.

"Oh, you are the blizzard's daughter all right," Tierra said, exasperation giving way to a somewhat grudging pride. She kissed Ilize lightly on the lips. After a moment's further consideration, Tierra kissed her again, not lightly at all. Inside her heavy furs Ilize's body radiated warmth all the way to her smallest finger, her remotest toe. At the front of the sled Neva trilled impatiently in her throat.

"And," Tierra said, "your foolishness seems to be contagious. The dogs, as usual, have more sense." She helped Ilize step up out of the drift and onto the sled and, aided undoubtedly by the snow eagle's outstretched wings, they returned to Tierra's home far more quickly than they had left it.

Once inside, Tierra vanished silently through the back door. Ilize thought to follow, but must first dry her dogs and pick ice balls from between their furry toes. As she finished, Tierra reappeared with supper, all the more welcome because it was dusk already and they had forgone lunch. Like last night's meal it was a miracle: a rich cassoulet of game birds that could not live in these latitudes. Both Ilize and Tierra ate with relish.

"We must try again tomorrow," Ilize said when they were done.

"No," said Tierra, collecting their bowls from Sax and Neva, who had licked them clean.

"What do you mean, no?"

"No," Tierra repeated. "As you could not pass today, you will not pass tomorrow, or the next day or the next, or any time until light and dark balance on the rim of the year."

"But I am the blizzard's daughter!" Ilize cried. "I want to find my father!"

"And so you shall, if you are patient," Tierra said firmly. "But believe me, without me beside you, you will not get half as far as we did today."

"Who are you anyway?" Ilize muttered.

Tierra spread her arms to indicate the circular room: the stove, the hearth, the blankets and furs, the looms taking the place of furniture. "As you see," she said.

"Hah," said Ilize.

"You and your dogs may stay here till the equinox," Tierra said. "I live a solitary life and am not much company for a young person like yourself; still, it has been many years since I visited south of the Great North River, and I would enjoy hearing how those lands fare these days."

Likely they haven't changed a bit, Ilize thought, even if it were centuries since you saw them last. Each year is just like the next and the one preceding. But she said no such thing, for in her mind a plan was coalescing. She would not wait till spring equinox, not for this odd hermit's sake or even for the snow eagle. "Perhaps I will stay," she said. "It seems foolish to spend weeks driving south again, only to return with the spring."

So she made up her bed again by the hearth, and fell asleep with her dogs curled up beside her.

She woke in the dark from a dream of dancing: her sister Anno played the bones while six circles of young men and women whirled around the dancing ground at the center of their village. Swirling costumes and flying beribboned hair vanished when Ilize opened her eyes; the driving rhythm of the bones did not. Tierra sat at a loom—not the white-on-white tapestry at the end but the one beside it—sending her shuttle through the threads while her foot worked an unseen pedal. Clackety clack, clackety clackety clackety clack! Sourceless light enveloped her, its apex above her head. And Ilize's dogs sat at the weaver's side, Neva on the left, Sax on the right, watching her raptly.

I could escape right now, Ilize thought. *I could creep up behind her and strangle her as she weaves.*

The mere idea turned her stomach and left a raw hollow in her throat. Humans might kill animals, for food, and animals humans, in self-defense, but for one person to kill another? This was the worst of horrors. Killing had no part in Ilize's plan to find her father.

But Ilize did rise, draw one blanket around her, and go to stand behind Tierra as she wove. Tierra's hair cascaded heavily over her shoulders to well below her waist. It smelled of woodsmoke and, faintly, of almonds. The moving thread was sunny green, but the newest rows were a somber greenish brown, like spring grass struggling through mud. Ilize studied the whole work over Tierra's shoulder. The pattern nagged at her: she should recognize the pattern, shouldn't she, the nubbly gray shape in the upper left, flecked with black and white; the silver-blue line that undulated down from the top; the lower right field, whose faintly discernible squares recalled Jehan's biggest quilt.

"So?" said Tierra, not pausing in her work.

Ilize parted Tierra's hair and kissed the back of her neck. The skin was musky and warm and feathered with tiny black hairs that tickled her lips.

"So," said Tierra. Her hands slowed and came to a halt. The tip of Ilize's tongue found the knob between Tierra's shoulder blades and brushed back and forth across it. "Do you know what you ask for?" she asked.

"Of course," Ilize whispered, smiling.

Tierra knew otherwise but rose nonetheless. She gazed deep into Ilize's dark eyes and saw far more there than Ilize guessed. Then she slid her shuttle hand around Ilize's neck, her fingers combing the pale and tangled hair that glowed in the faint light. Ilize tried to turn her head but could not. Deliberately Tierra kissed the center of the triangle at the base of Ilize's throat. Ilize swallowed hard: this was nothing like the fumbling trysts of growing up.

"Will you," Tierra asked, her eyes laughing though her mouth did not, "hide behind that blanket forever?"

Words failed Ilize. She let the blanket slide to the ground. Tierra touched her breasts—small as a boy's, one of last winter's partners had marveled—and let her hand slide down Ilize's flat belly and around her hip to buttocks that weren't small at all. "Ahh," Tierra breathed out loud.

This was a bad idea, Ilize thought, *it's stupid, I don't want* ... But she could neither muster words nor pull away, for Tierra's arms held her and Tierra's hands stroked down her back. Ilize's thighs thrummed and between them opened to the promise of touch. Tierra's fingers teased her from behind: Tierra was tall, her reach long. How small Ilize felt, how far, far from home.

Finally Tierra drew back, and Ilize watched her undress, slowly, thong by thong, button by button. At the sight of Tierra's breasts, Ilize flushed hot from cheeks to belly. Her right hand reached out, cupped left breast, caressed the nipple with a thumb. Her lips followed, kissed, licked, drew back. She sank to her knees to unknot the sash that held Tierra's leather leggings—mercifully it yielded easily to her fingers—and worked them down to her bare feet.

Abruptly Ilize stood, before the scent of sex went to her head, and she remained standing, heedless, till Tierra nodded toward her rumpled pile of furs and blankets. As she knelt down, Ilize recalled her intent: to invite herself through the barely discernible door at the back, where Tierra slept and worked who knew what other wonders. Hah! As likely to direct the rain once it starts to fall! She sensed movement nearby and startled; Neva and Sax settled into their places just beyond her bed and each laid head on forepaws, watching.

In a moment Ilize was watching them just as intently, stretched out on her belly while Tierra stood above. What so intrigued the older woman that she could not lie down too, as Ilize desperately wished she would? Surely she could not know . . . ? But she must know how Ilize longed to writhe on the blankets, to ease the anticipation that flowered below her belly—must know that, even before Ilize whispered, "Please . . ."

Tierra knelt down and slid a hand between Ilize's lean and muscled thighs, teased her cunt with two fingers.

"Yes!" Ilize breathed, her body grasping for more touch.

Tierra swatted Ilize's bottom with her free hand. "Patience, child, patience!" she rebuked her guest. "You asked who I am? Now you shall find out—but I warn you, I take no pleasure in haste."

"No, Lady," murmured Ilize.

So Ilize rose to her knees and turned, tasting, at Tierra's invitation, her own desire on Tierra's fingers. Then with tongue and lips she traced Tierra's wrist, her smooth inner forearm, the sinewy crook of her elbow, and the earthy pungence above it. She sucked at Tierra's breasts and abandoned them with profound reluctance—and Tierra's prodding—to follow downward the faint crease in her belly. Tierra tasted like a garden so exuberantly lush that particular flavors could not be discerned, only savored.

Slowly, slowly, Ilize told herself, though it was like holding her dogs back when they wanted to fly. She spread her hands around Tierra's buttocks and with the merest tip of her tongue circled Tierra's cunt, slipping inward by infinitesimal degrees—"Ah!" said Tierra, shifting her hips—until she was smelling, tasting, breathing the woman's molten soul, or so it seemed. For a moment she forgot entirely what to do, to coax that rising heat to its surging crescendo.

Tierra moved. Without remembering how she got there, Ilize lay on her back, head in Tierra's lap, Tierra's tongue probing her mouth. Tierra moved over Ilize's face, down her breasts and across her belly like a lazy snake, while Ilize shadowed her every move. Then the snake struck, kindling fire and quenching it, kindling and quenching, till fire exploded, deep within the earth, and spread outward and upward in wave after wave. Outward and downward came the mirror fire, and ghost lights danced in the darkest corners of the room.

When Ilize woke, the room's only light came from the banked embers in the stove. Tierra slept on, their bodies touching from belly to knee. Neva rose to her feet and stretched from black nose to plumy tail, with Sax following suit. Time to realize her plan, Ilize thought, though nagging at all her senses was the notion that spending the rest of the winter making love with Tierra was far more appealing than venturing out into the wild blizzards' land. Her bones were liquid, she felt unsteady on her feet.

❦ Stars Inside Her

I am the blizzard's daughter, she reminded herself and got up. Silently she dressed and found her ready pack and, beside it, the canvas bag that held the dogs' harness. All that remained was to slip out the door; if that didn't wake Tierra, surely she would not notice Ilize's walking round outside to the overhang that sheltered the sled, or harnessing the dogs, or gliding northward over the snow.

Where was the snow eagle? Ilize had last seen it in its customary place, in the front of the sled. It must still be there. Unless Tierra had brought it indoors, for reasons of her own . . . ? No matter, thought Ilize, confident that the snow eagle would not stray far from her. She scratched Sax's ears, then Neva's. The dogs slipped toward the door.

Light exploded behind her. Ilize whirled around. Tierra stood, magnificent, her brown body shimmering. "Where," she asked, "are you going?"

"To seek my father," answered Ilize, for evasion was pointless, and impossible.

"You will not," said Tierra.

Pack slung over one shoulder, Ilize took a defiant step toward the door. In an instant Tierra blocked her way, looming even larger than she had before.

"You are a spoiled child," Tierra said, "and an ignorant one. Go to him now and the blizzard will leave you freezing in the waste."

Nearly choking on her fear, Ilize stepped forward again. She raised her hand, not knowing what her hand intended; Tierra caught it in her own. Ilize felt the heat from Tierra's palm and fingers rushing down her own arm into her shoulder, into her breast, which glowed under her clothing. "You can't keep me here!" she cried.

"Can I not?" A smile played on Tierra's lips. "More, I can make you forget you ever wanted to leave, or why."

"My dogs will not let you stop me!"

In response Tierra called them by name: "Sax? Neva?" And the two flanked her and sat, tails wagging, waiting for her next command. Ilize was furious. She glanced around the room and abruptly bolted toward the penultimate loom, dropping her pack and drawing her knife.

"Fool!" hissed Tierra, blocking her with absurd ease, deflecting her rage back into her body, where it quickly turned to desire, racing like heat lightning along her jaw-line, down her throat, and shimmering in her breasts. Ilize felt the heartbeat, the pulse of Tierra's body, steadying the erratic throbbing of her own. Even their breaths were synchronizing. Ilize yanked away and crouched warily by the hearth, Tierra straightened. For an instant her hair streamed from the room's rocky ceiling to its grassy floor.

"Truly you are the blizzard's daughter," Tierra said, "ready to destroy without a thought for consequence."

"That's a lie!" Ilize spat.

"Is it?" At once Ilize's knife was in Tierra's right hand. "Is this not your knife?"

"Bewitched by you!"

"But yours."

"Yes."

"And did you not aim to slash the warp and weft of my tapestry, with no thought in heart or mind but to thwart me?"

She had indeed, though now that hot anger had sub-
sided the attempt seemed not only futile but childish.
With her silence, she accepted the charge as true.

"I won't do it again," Ilize whispered. "I promise."

"A small amend," Tierra roared, "for the harm you
nearly did!"

Tierra's fury singed the dross from her. Ilize shed her
parka, her sweaters and boots and leggings. Naked she lay
at Tierra's feet. "Truly I won't," she pleaded. "Believe me,
please believe me!"

"I should cast you into the snow, stupid girl," Tierra
said, no longer angry. "That's what you wanted, isn't it?"

"I want to find my father, that's all," Ilize replied.

"And who is your father, and what use will he have
for you—have you thought of that?" Tierra paused. "Of
course not. You never do, all you blizzard's daughters, and
your mothers are the worse off for it."

Ilize had assumed all along that she would return to
Jehan's house by corn harvest at the latest.

"I will show you," said Tierra, "what you would
have destroyed. Get up."

Ilize rose and followed Tierra to the next-to-last
loom, the one at which the weaver had been working so
much earlier that night. There was the rocky gray patch,
like volcanic hills, and the frozen river, and the widening
swath of evergreen billowing out from it like a festival
dancer's skirt. Why, I'm seeing land, not tapestry at all!

Tierra stood behind her, breasts against Ilize's shoulder blades, belly against back. Tierra's hands covered
Ilize's ears and focused her eyes. Ilize saw: the fields east
and south of her village, snow fallen high on the perime-
ters but merely dusting the ground where people dwelt.

Of course! Wasn't that the Running Wolf River, tributary of the Great North? Now she recognized its jagged fork, wild rapids to the west, waterfall to the east, just before it became the abundant river that nourished her people's fields—and sometimes flooded low-lying barns and houses.

"It's . . ." Ilize began.

Tierra's hands pressed more firmly on Ilize's temples.

"I see people, not many people, but some, fishing by the river."

"So," said Tierra. "And the river is not frozen all the way across, like the Great North, and the paths between houses are clear, and—this you cannot see—the earth remains warm and fertile under the snow, and there countless animals are sleeping till spring."

Ilize understood. She glanced toward the rightmost loom, with its vast white-on-white weaving, and shivered.

"You begin to understand," Tierra said, letting her hands fall to Ilize's shoulders.

"Who are you?" Ilize whispered.

"Ask not who but *what*," said the weaver. She draped Ilize with a blanket, found a hooded robe for herself, and set the copper kettle on the stove to heat. Ilize progressed counter-sunwise around the room, studying the other tapestries. Though she saw no people, she thought she discerned square fields in one, straddling both sides of a river narrower and deeper (how did she know that?) than the Running Wolf, and rolling rocky hills, where sheep might graze.

"I am not alone but one of several on the marches of the blizzards' land," Tierra resumed, standing by the stove, "who keep the memories of earth and water alive. There, at the end?" She thrust her chin toward the white weaving. "I lost that one, for now. The snow piled too deep, the ice too thick; the deer went southward and finally the remnants of the people followed. Blizzards feed on cold and take fire for their mortal enemy. We contain them during the months that offer them most sustenance—two or three may escape to work their havoc each winter, and one or two may walk abroad in human form. This much can be endured. Not so a legion of storms, one after another."

"And my mother?"

"Ah, Jehan! What a triumph it would have been, to leave her a frozen shell of herself."

Jehan a frozen shell? Ilize laughed out loud. Jehan's warmth drew all to her, Jehan's care saved lambs that others gave up on, Jehan's faith inspired all to carry buckets from the river when rain was scarce, and to dig ditches to the fields where the most fragile crops grew. No one understood how Jehan could have borne such a cool, pale-haired daughter as Ilize.

"Truly," said Tierra. "Jehan remained Jehan, and... Ilize... must chart her own course. Not, however, when others' lives are at stake."

"What," Ilize asked, "have you done with the snow eagle?"

"The snow eagle is as safe in my keeping as it was in your mother's," said Tierra.

"I will wait until spring," Ilize said. Neva stretched out beside the hearth with a satisfied groan. Sax sat as if waiting for the water to boil.

"You will," said Tierra, "wait until spring."

And so she did, and the story of where her destiny next took her must wait for another time.

CONTRIBUTORS

Katya Andreevna lives in New York City. Her work has appeared in *Best American Erotica 1996*, *Best Lesbian Erotica 1997 The New Worlds of Women*, and *Pillow Talk: Lesbian Stories Between the Covers*. She loves Slavic fairy tales and has based her story in this collection on one of the ancient Russian byliny.

Kat Beyer lives in Santa Cruz, California. She works in Silicon Valley. The rest of the time she writes, draws, trains in Aikido, studies languages, pretends to play the guitar and the djimbe, and reads too much Jane Austen. She took her M.A. in Medieval History from the University of St. Andrews, Scotland. She has been up Arthur's Seat.

Reina Delacroix is the pen name of a shy, quiet information architect, living in Northern Virginia with her cats, George and Shen T'ien; her precious pet Michael, and her loyal Wolf, Marc. When she can manage to get away from the computer, she likes both martial arts and swing dancing. She has published many other stories with Circlet Press.

❧ Stars Inside Her

Imat is an award-winning poet, photographer, and fantasy writer. She is a cultural anthropologist who makes a living working for the opera and a non-profit legal organization. Currently she is working on a poetry collection entitled *Venus Was Never Wet*. After years of writing short erotica stories by request, she will soon be launching a custom erotica web site where stories will be written to order.

Jana McCall writes, edits, proofreads, and enjoys life, not necessarily in that order. One story of hers, "Self Made Woman," appeared in *S/M Futures*. She still is a fervent lurker on the Internet, and is seriously thinking of competing as an extreme web surfer in the next Techno-Olympics.

Stefanie Tatalias Phillips began telling stories when she learned to talk. Since then, she is often asked if the tale is true. She doesn't think that her BA, her resume, or anything else validates a story more than how the reader feels after sharing her sliver of reality.

Teresa Noelle Roberts is a poet, fiction writer and Middle Eastern dancer, but earns her living as a fundraiser for a Boston cultural organization. Her hobbies include collecting redheads and confusing mundanes. She has no tattoos.

Susanna J. Sturgis, during two decades of involvement in the fantasy/science fiction field as bookseller, reviewer, editor, and cheerleader for the James Tiptree Jr. Memorial Award, keeps swearing that she "doesn't write the stuff." "The Blizzard's Daughter" and stories published in *Night Bites* and *Night Shade* (both from Seal Press) suggest that this is not entirely true. She lives on Martha's Vineyard, Mass., where she makes her living as a freelance editor, sings in the Island Community Chorus, and spends as much time around horses as possible. Her dog, Rhodry Malamutt, wants everyone to know that he looks a lot like Ilize's dog Sax.

Cecilia Tan founded Circlet Press in 1992 and has edited dozens of anthologies of erotic fantasy and science fiction. Her own writing has graced the pages of both *Penthouse* magazine and *Ms.*, *Best Lesbian Erotica*, *Best American Erotica*, and *Isaac Asimov's Science Fiction Magazine*. Her collection of short stories, BLACK FEATHERS: *Erotic Dreams*, was published by HarperCollins. She is currently writing an erotic work entitled *The Book of Want*.

Jessy Luanni Wolf has published stories as Jessie Lynda Lasnover, Jessy Luanni Blackburn, and Jessy Luanni Wolf, in *Lesbian Bedtime Stories* (Tough Dove), *Lesbian Adventure Stories* (Tough Dove), *Dykescapes* (Alyson), *Lesbian Short Fiction* (Women of Diversity), *Leatherwomen II* (Rosebud), *The Lesbian Erotic Cookbook* (Daughters of the Moon) and *The New Worlds of Women* (Circlet). She is a lesbian, mother, grandmother, pagan, writer, teacher, feminist, vegetarian, and zine publisher of *Coffy Time Blues*.

ACKNOWLEDGEMENTS

Many people have helped to make this book and Circlet Press a success, and I cannot possibly thank all of them here. But I'll try.

Thanks to our unflagging crew of interns, including, but never limited to, Jessica, Susannah, Alison, Netanel, Jess, Alex, Eric, Liz, Jennifer, and the others whose tenure the creation of this book has spanned.

Thanks to our various techno-angels, including corwin, Steve, John, and the Ranch crew, for all the computer miracles they've created. And let's not forget Eric for saving my back by moving boxes, and J.B. and Ted for the airconditioner. I wouldn't have lived through the summer without you guys.

Thanks to Nancy Bereano, Carol Seajay, David Wilk and the crew at LPC, and everyone else who has helped us weather the rocky waters in the book industry.

ABOUT THE PUBLISHER

Circlet Press was founded in 1992 to publish works of fantasy and science fiction that were considered too erotic to be published by the mainstream genre presses. *Telepaths Don't Need Safewords* by Cecilia Tan was the press' first chapbook, followed soon after by *Mate* by Lauren P. Burka, and two anthologies, *Forged Bonds* and *Feline Fetishes*. (All four chapbooks are now available in an omnibus volume, *Tales from the Erotic Edge*.) Full size trade paperback anthologies soon followed, including a series of erotic vampire books (*Blood Kiss*, *Erotica Vampirica*, *Cherished Blood*), and those focused on gay male sexuality (*Wired Hard*, *Wired Hard 2*) and SM/leather/fetishes (*S/M Futures*, *S/M Pasts*, *Fetish Fantastic*). Circlet then branched out into non-erotic fantasy and science fiction with queer themes with the imprint The Ultra Violet Library, which has featured, to date, *The Drag Queen of Elfland* by Lawrence Schimel, *Things Invisible to See*, edited by Lawrence Schimel, and *Through A Brazen Mirror* by Delia Sherman.

For more information about Circlet Press, upcoming anthologies, internship opportunities, and more, please visit us on the World Wide Web at www.circlet.com.